A *High-Country*

CHRISTMAS

ROMANCE COLLECTION

BOOKS BY DAVALYNN SPENCER

Historical

THE FRONT RANGE BRIDES SERIES

Mail-Order Misfire – series prequel
An Improper Proposal - Book 1
An Unexpected Redemption - Book 2
An Impossible Price – Book 3 (coming Spring 2020)

THE CAÑON CITY CHRONICLES SERIES

Loving the Horseman - Book 1
Straight to My Heart - Book 2
Romancing the Widow - Book 3
The Cañon City Chronicles - complete collection

Novella Collections

"The Wrangler's Woman" - *The Cowboy's Bride Collection*
"*The Snowbound Bride*" - *The 12 Brides of Christmas*
"The Columbine Bride" - *The 12 Brides of Summer*

High-Country Christmas Novellas

Snow Angel
Just in Time for Christmas

Contemporary

The Miracle Tree

Stay in touch via my quarterly author update and receive a free novella when you sign up here: http://eepurl.com/xa81D

Just in Time

FOR CHRISTMAS

Trust in the Lord, and do good;
so shalt thou dwell in the land,
and verily thou shalt be fed.

Psalm 37:3

CHAPTER 1

Autumn 1875
The Catamounts, El Paso County, Colorado Territory

T he chair tipped beneath her boots.

Abigale fanned her arms, fighting for balance in the barn's drafty loft, but the chair tipped further. She dove into the hay pile, cringing as wood splintered on the barn floor twelve feet below.

That was the second kitchen chair she'd lost in three days.

Rolling to her back, she looked up at the leaky roof. If she didn't know better, she'd think Pop had deliberately taken his shotgun to it. But she *did* know better. He'd been up in years, not out of his mind.

A tear escaped and slid to her temple. If she hadn't gone back to school after Mams passed last year, she could have helped him more, and he might not have worked himself underneath that marker in the family plot.

She stood and brushed hay from her hair and clothes, then kicked the wooden boxes she'd stacked in the loft. Not exactly the most stable foundation for balancing a chair.

None of her classes at Wolfe Hall had prepared her for patching a roof without the aid of a ladder, and she didn't relish the thought of climbing up on top of the barn, ladder or no. The loft was full of summer hay, so she'd have feed enough for the horses and milk cow, but only if she could keep the snow out.

And it'd soon be snowing by the foot, for the aspens had already turned.

So did the irony. Pop had called her his Aspen-gal ever since he and Mams took her in as an orphaned six-year-old.

"Just a few letters difference is all, for a pretty little gal with yella hair," he'd said.

His nickname had changed everything.

As sure as the white-barked trees slipped from green to shimmering gold each fall, a timid, lonely child transformed into one who believed she could do anything she set her mind to.

Unless it involved heights.

Slowly descending the makeshift ladder nailed to the barn wall, she studied the rungs and how they were spaced. Why couldn't she build one just like it on the outside of the barn, a rung at a time? It might be safer than her balancing act in the loft, and less costly. She had only two kitchen chairs left.

Below her, Chester yapped and wagged his encouragement. Not that she *saw* him. She simply knew that his happy bark meant a fanning tail. Looking down made things worse. If she didn't look down, she didn't have to think about how high up she was.

As the box stalls rose into her peripheral vision, she chanced a peek. Sure enough, Chester's feathery tail swept the air.

"Good boy." She stepped to blessed *terra firma* and rubbed the dog's russet-colored back. "What would I do without your encouragement?"

Pieces of broken chair lay scattered around her, as well as the fallen board she'd tried to nail on the underside of the roof, and she tossed them on a heap of scrap lumber in Pop's work room. A neat stack of shingles from the Windsor lumber mill waited for her to be reasonable and use them to replace those that had blown off or worn through. But that meant nailing them on from the outside.

As always, Pop's intentions had been good. But this time they simply came too late.

A shelf along one wall held most of his tools, aside from those that hung from nails above. Leather punches, awls, hammers, a saw. Everything looked just as he'd left it, as if he'd walk in the door any minute and ask what she was doing. Sinking into her memories of the tall, robust man, she smelled the pipe smoke that clung to his plaid wool shirts. Saw the crinkles at the corners of his laughing eyes, the shock of white hair that helped her spot him from a distance if he wasn't wearing his old brown hat.

It hung from a nail by a spare harness collar and she plopped it on her head. Fitting as poorly as ever, it made her feel like Pop was nearby, encouraging her on like Chester. It made her feel less lonely.

Rather than return to the loft for the hammer she'd left behind, she chose another one from Pop's collection, shoved it in the belt holding up his trousers, and pocketed a handful of nails. After arming herself with several shorter pieces from the scrap pile, she cinched her determination, and marched out to the mountain side of the barn.

Chester followed.

"This is a simple task—hold the board against the barn and drive a nail in each end."

The dog dropped to his haunches as if expecting a show.

Abigale inspected the wooden siding, chose a narrow section between two vertical boards that created a shallow space, and nailed the first slat across it at knee height. The second one she hammered in level with her waist, and the third one she set even with her shoulders. Pleased with her work so far, she tugged on the rungs, testing their hold.

So far so good.

Craning her head back, she looked up. Way up past the barn into the gray-bellied clouds.

With her fingers clenched like a corset around the slats, she shut her eyes, climbed up to the second rung and back down.

Chester barked.

"Thank you. Now if you'll just follow me up, you can carry a shingle in your mouth."

And it would take her a month to patch the roof. That would never do, for snow was sure to fly tonight. Besides, Chester didn't climb ladders. But she could rig a rope pully and haul the shingles that way. Or fashion a sling across her back and carry them with her. Wouldn't Miss Butterfield be impressed with her ingenuity?

Abigale snorted—a most unladylike habit she'd been temporarily shamed out of by the Wolfe Hall head mistress. But up here in the high country where the air was crisp and bracing, and the gun-metal sky so low she could touch it, such a rebellious gesture felt somehow liberating.

She mustered her nerve by considering the three mouths she had to feed that now grazed on winter-dry grass in the near pasture. Clearly, no one had felt compelled to take a couple of old horses and Ernestine home for the winter.

You'd think someone would have fetched them, someone like the Holts from the next ranch over.

Memories flickered by, all the hours she'd tagged along with their son Seth. But what would he want with a couple of broken-down saddle horses and a dry cow?

Chester, on the other hand, still had a few good years in him. At the funeral, Pastor Meeks had agreed to take him home. Maybe the old dog had come back of his own accord.

Like she had.

She gathered more slat-like pieces from the scrap pile, slid them into her belt, and started up the so-called ladder.

A snowflake landed on her nose.

Nooo, not yet!

A drumroll tumbled, but she refused to look at the peak rising behind her. She'd witnessed thundersnow once as a child, a phenomenon that Pop said required precise conditions to occur. She didn't need those precise conditions now. She needed to patch the roof and preserve the hay.

Pressed close as she was against the outside of the barn, she couldn't see the wide park spreading out to the east, but she sensed the gathering storm and felt the cloud ceiling drop even lower.

Ignoring the next few flakes, she extended her ladder by three more slats, inspiring perseverance. She stepped up on one slat with another at waist level, appreciating the semblance of security. With wooden piece in hand against the barn's side, she set a nail at one end, and pounded it in. Emboldened by the minute, she finished another set of three and climbed up to start on the next, and then the next.

A thunderous crash set the barn trembling, and she flinched. The hammer slipped from her hand, her fingers from the rung, and her heart lurched to her throat as bottomless space opened beneath her.

~

The gelding reared at the close hit, but Seth Holt kept his seat, gathering Coop with a steady hand and a calm voice.

Thundersnow, Old Man Millerton had called it, though it still struck Seth odd when lightning and snow hit together.

Go now.

The words shuttled through him like a whisper through an aspen stand, unspoken but not unheard. He didn't want to go now—he wanted to go home. Cutting straight across the grassland, he'd make the ranch in a couple of hours, and escape most of the snow likely to fall closer to the mountain.

Go now.

He yanked his hat down and blamed his ma. Somehow she'd planted that insistent knowing of what he should do even though he didn't want to do it.

The Millerton place would soon be up for sale, most of the livestock already gone. So was Abigale. He'd seen her at the funeral last week but held back when everyone crowded around her. He waited so long that by the time he saw his way clear, the preacher was handing her up to the stagecoach.

Just as gutsy as she'd always been. Seth would sooner ride Coop over the pass bareback than bounce all the way down to Colorado Springs in a stage.

Reining in, he listened. Waited. Tension etched the air, building for another thunder roll. Snow fell straight down, silent and dry. But no more gut-tugs. Nothing.

He unlashed his slicker from behind his saddle, shrugged it on, and turned Coop toward the Millertons'. Two tugs were enough. The worst that could happen was he'd get snowed in and spend the night in Pop Millerton's sagging barn. The best thing that could happen was no stock to drive back to his folks' place tomorrow.

Another crack shattered the falling sky, and Coop quivered beneath him. Mountain storms often rolled up without much warning, and every rancher, farmer, and lumberman around Summit Park knew it. But this storm had stalked in like a catamount, waiting till the last minute to cut a lightning swath through the falling flakes. He had just enough time to make Millertons' before full dark dropped on him.

Coop resisted, but good mount that he was, he lowered his head and plodded into the storm.

An hour later, the wind had picked up, and Millertons' old barn rose against the gusts, shoulders hunched and gathering snow. Seth rode around the south end, prepared to jump down and swing one of the double doors wide. But he checked the reins in surprise at the open door, then urged Coop inside.

"Easy, boy. We're good here. Easy." He patted the gelding's neck, murmuring low as the horse blew and shook his head. Another lightning whip and Seth wondered if the old barn would come down on them both. But it stood strong, its giant timbers reminiscent of the man who had raised them more than thirty years ago. Least that's what Seth's pa had told him.

Wind kicked up another notch, the sky bellied out, and snow blew in through the doors and windows. He unsaddled Coop and led him to a box stall, counting on the confined space to comfort the animal. He thought a dog barked, but that was crazy. Surely someone had taken old Chester. Wouldn't have been Abigale, since she'd gone back to that fancy girls' school in Denver, where she likely had a handful of beaus.

A frantic yap pulled him around. Chester stood in the doorway, his red coat thick with snow.

Seth closed the stall door and approached the dog, wondering if it remembered him. "Come on, Chester. Get on in here."

He reached for the dog's collar, but it stepped back and growled.

Seth hadn't heard of any rabid animals in the area, but he eyed his rifle scabbard just the same.

The dog barked again. No tail wag. Just a hard bark and harder glare. It trotted out of view, then returned, stopping farther out. Another bark.

Fool dog.

Seth stepped out under the eaves and checked the pasture. Three horses and a milk cow crowded the fence corner farthest from the storm's approach, but the dog had gone in the opposite direction.

The skin on the back of Seth's necked crawled. He eased out to the mountain side of the barn and peeked around the corner. A light wagon sat close by, one he didn't remember seeing before. Beyond it, Chester pawed at a snowy mound.

The dog ran toward him, barked, and returned to the heap.

The chill on Seth's neck crawled into his scalp. Screwing his hat down, he ran out and scooped up what turned out to be a body, and carried it inside.

He laid the body on a straw pile and rolled it over. When he took off his hat for a better look, his heart slammed against his ribs, and the sensation set him back on his heels.

A wide belt cinched the small waist, and thin wood slats sprouted around it. Snow clung to a long pale braid, and unmistakable female features contradicted men's clothing.

Wiping snow from a faint scar across the left eyebrow, Seth recalled a stubborn twelve-year-old he'd warned not to shimmy down the north side of Aspen Falls.

He felt for a pulse at neck and wrist, then leaned in close. Close enough to kiss her like he'd wanted to since they were old enough to know better. Instead, he held his breath until he felt hers against his face.

"Abigale Millerton. What in the world are you doing here in your grandfather's clothes, covered with snow, and out cold as a cut tree?"

CHAPTER 2

The wind howled a promise of deep drifts by morning. Seth tossed an armful of hay into Coop's feed box, wrapped Abigale in his slicker, and, holding her close against him, ducked his head and ran for the log house.

Chester didn't miss a trick. He was in the door before it closed, shaking snow off his back and onto the entry where Seth had always left his muddy boots or dusty chaps or whatever he'd worn that drew a look from Abigale's grandmother. The dog trailed across the big open room and stopped in front of the stone fireplace, where it sat and looked Seth's way.

"First things first." He carried Abigale to the old leather sofa set at right angles to the fireplace and pushed one of her grandmother's fancy pillows under her head. His hand came away sticky, and his throat clinched as he fingered a sizeable lump on the back of her head. Unwrapping his slicker was like unfolding a bean burrito, though Abigale Millerton was a heap prettier than a pile of beans.

Lord a'mighty, how was he gonna get her outta those wet clothes? If she chilled, there was no telling what might happen.

He squatted next to her and leaned in close. "Abigale—wake up."

Not a peep.

He cupped her shoulder and gave it a light shake. "Abigale, you in there?"

Chester barked and Seth nearly jumped out of his boots. He swiveled toward the dog, then back again on the off chance the noise had startled Abigale awake.

No such luck.

He couldn't let her lie there in Pop's snow-soaked clothes, but his only alternative scared him more than a polecat in the outhouse. What if she came to while he was … well, while he was …

He shot upright and grabbed one end of the sofa and turned the whole thing till it faced the hearth, hugging it close. Then he set to building a fire and in no time had a hearty blaze going. Chester stretched out with a groan and laid his head on his paws, watching.

"Sure. Just make yourself at home."

The dog raised his head and stared at him.

"All right. It's your home and you helped me find her. But now what am I supposed to do?"

With a heavy sigh, Chester dropped his head and closed his eyes.

One thing Seth knew for certain, he wasn't leaving Abigale alone and unconscious with only a dog for company.

He'd been in this house more times than he could count and remembered his way around. Upstairs in the Millertons' bedroom, he went through the bureau drawers until he found some old clothes of Pop's that might fit him, including extra socks. He took two quilts off the brass bed, then stopped in what used to be Abigale's room.

Still was, it looked like, for a fancy traveling suit lay over the back of a chair. High top button up shoes sat next to it, and a little hat and some other strange contraption perched on the seat. Leaving such puzzling under-riggings alone, he dug through a chest of drawers, hunting dry clothes. He hit the jackpot with trousers she used to ride in, a shirt, and more socks.

Socks he could handle. The thought of anything else tied his insides in knots.

He tromped down the stairs, making as much of a racket as possible in hopes it'd wake Abigale. But she just lay there. The fire had already warmed the room considerably, and he draped the clothes and quilts over a big stuffed chair, then added more wood to the blaze.

Chester sighed with contentment.

Seth started with Abigale's feet, pulling off familiar brown riding boots. They were soaked through, so he set them on the hearth and went to work on her stockings. *Hose*, he thought they were called. Dark, thin things that clung to her like a second skin. Thinking about her skin made *his* skin twitch, and as fast as he could, he pushed up the wet trouser legs and pulled off the clingy things. Then he tugged the wool socks onto her pale feet and wondered if all the blood in her body had gone to her kidneys. She was as fair and white as aspen bark.

Coffee. He needed coffee. Maybe the smell would wake her up.

But the heavy wet pants worried him more than propriety. He reached for the wide belt at her waist and unfastened the buckle, watching her face all the while for any sign that she was coming around. Even the pieces of wood that fell from the belt were soaked, and they went on the hearth with her stockings.

He covered her with the heaviest quilt and pushed the edges under her shoulders to hold it in place for what he was about to do. Then with a prayer that she wouldn't wake up in the middle of his next move, he reached under the quilt, grabbed the bottom of the trousers—one leg in each hand—and pulled.

It was easier than he'd hoped.

After laying the pants out on the hearth, he added more wood, fired up the cook stove for coffee, and stood at the hearth holding the other quilt wide like wings. When the backing heated up enough that he could smell it, he draped it over the first quilt, then tucked it in around her feet and legs.

That was as far as he'd go, but at least he'd gotten that far. It'd be up to the good Lord to keep her wet shirt from chilling her lungs.

He brought a pan of cold water and a rag to the hearth, where he knelt beside her. Carefully he lifted her shoulders, holding her against his chest with one arm as he pressed the wet rag against the back of her head. She'd grown a goose egg for sure, but blood wasn't running. Just a scrape, it seemed. But she'd hit hard, and it frightened him more than anything had in a long while.

He'd always worried where Abigale Millerton was concerned, the way she'd get an idea in her head and take off. This time she was wearing that idea, and a good-sized lump it was. He eased her back down.

Darkness wrapped around the house and the wind tied it down. He grabbed a lantern from a peg by the door, shrugged into his slicker and hat, and headed out. The animals needed to be in the barn with the doors shuttered.

Already snow drifted against the buildings and bowed the trees. Lantern light threw a yellow arc ahead as he trudged through the swirling white.

Three horses and a cow stood at the corral gate, backs to the wind.

Seth eased between the poles, crossed the corral, and slid the gate bar. All four snow-crusted critters trotted through and into the barn. After securing the gate, he tossed hay into stalls, made sure all the barn shutters were closed, and slid the long bar across the big double doors.

At the house, he walked around back to the chopping block, where he found an axe sunk in it. An old schoolbook had mentioned firewood warming a man twice, and he knew it to be true. Stacked wood hunkered dry beneath the eaves, and he set about unsticking the axe and splitting an armload.

As soon as he stepped inside the house, the aroma of fresh coffee set his stomach to rumbling for supper. He hung the lantern and stomped snow off his boots, hoping the noise would wake Abigale, but she didn't shoot up off the sofa screaming. Just as well.

Still holding the wood, he managed to wedge his boots off in a jack at the entry, then piled his load on the hearth stones. He hung his slicker on a peg by the door and pulled the big chair up close to the hearth where he fell into it. Abigale lay like the dead beside him. He sure hoped she wasn't.

Every muscle in his body threatened mutiny. He needed to get his wet clothes off too, but he propped his feet on the hearth and wiggled his toes. For just a second, he'd lay his head back and rest. A minute or two. Then he'd change and pour coffee, and maybe Abigale would wake up.

~

Abigale savored the smell of coffee almost more than the taste of it. She snuggled into her bed—or tried to, but it wasn't the same. Rather damp, the pillow hard. And her head hurt.

The snap of a burning log shot her eyes open, and it took her a moment to recognize the ceiling of her grandparents' home. *Her* home for most of her life. Of course. She'd come home. Left school early and … Another log broke, sparking her memory. She sat up and her head pounded like a smithy's hammer on an anvil. What was she doing in the great room?

Slowly she turned to the left toward the fire's warmth. She didn't remember building a fire. Rubbing her forehead, she connected with wet hair, then realized her shirt was wet. Her pulse kicked up and questions marched through her muddled thoughts.

Two quilts from her grandparents' bed covered her. She looked again toward the fire and this time saw two stockinged feet propped on the hearth, attached to long legs that led to Pop's wing-backed armchair.

Her attention fired back to the hearth and her grandfather's clothing spread out next to her stockings.

Her stockings!

Quickly she felt for her clothes and squelched a scream at finding only her wet shirt and unmentionables. The hammering in her temples intensified, and she pulled the quilts tighter around her.

Whose feet were stretched out there so close by? And why were her clothes on the hearth and not on her? And how'd they get there?

She couldn't contain her cry, and the long legs in Pop's chair shot someone straight up off the seat.

Seth Holt. Looking as startled as she felt.

Pressing into the sofa, she drew her legs up. What was he doing here and … No. *No.* She'd not even think such a thought. Seth was a gentleman.

Eyes dark, hair plastered to his head, he knelt beside her, relief and fear rushing across his features.

"Abi—gale." Stumbling over her name, he tried again. "Abigale. What are you doing here?"

"What are *you* doing here?

"I came to check for stragglers. Drive them home so they didn't starve."

"They won't starve. The loft is full of hay."

"You didn't answer my question." A deep line cut between his drawn brows, as if he'd warned her not to do something, then rescued her from it. The idea chafed her. She didn't need rescuing. She was perfectly capable of most things.

Shifting her knees to the side, she sat up straighter. "What happened?"

"I was hoping you could tell me." The line on his forehead smoothed. His shoulders eased, and that old light danced across his face like it did when they were children in a verbal tug o' war.

He rolled back on his heels and dropped to the floor with his legs crossed—one smooth movement he'd said he learned around chuck fires. Envious, she'd practiced the move in the privacy of her room but could never quite manage it. She'd also begrudged his freedom to ride out to the cow camps during branding. Pop and Mams said it was no place for a lady and wouldn't let her go.

"Abigale."

His voice had gentled, and it drew her back to the present, her gaze to the hearth.

"How'd Pop's britches get over there?"

Seth flushed red as an autumn apple and stood. "I couldn't very well let you catch your death. You were soaked clear through."

She narrowed her eyes. "You didn't answer *my* question."

The flush deepened to his personal color of mad she knew so well. "I didn't see anything 'cept your feet and legs. I mean limbs."

He crushed an oath under his breath as he reached back for Pop's trousers and tossed them at her.

"I pulled these off underneath that first quilt you're wearin'."

Abigale had spent more than a decade growing up with Seth Holt—swimming in the same holes, exploring the same waterfall, riding bareback across the open parks. She believed him. "Thank you."

"You're welcome." He relocated to the end of the sofa, more of a man than the over-grown boy she'd left behind two years ago. She hadn't seen much of him during her brief visits, not even at the funeral, but studying his profile now revealed that he'd traded his boyish face for a leaner, stronger jawline. His shoulders were broader, his hands sun-browned and capable. She shifted uncomfortably at the thought of him carrying her inside and … *helping* her.

He picked up one of the slats laid out on the hearth. "You had these tucked into Pop's belt. What were you doing out by the barn?"

Memory flooded back, and with it, pride at progress toward her goal. Her success at not looking down.

"I was making a ladder, nailing slats to the barn and climbing as I went so I could patch the roof. The loft is full of hay and the roof is full of holes."

He looked at her then, his features settled, calmer. "But you're afraid of heights, Aspen-gal."

The endearment pinched her already bruised heart, and she studied the quilt's log-cabin pattern. The quilt from upstairs. Typical of his thoughtfulness. He'd never teased her about her embarrassing secret, and he wasn't teasing her now.

"That's not why I fell. The lightning—it was so close and the crash so loud, it surprised me. I lost my balance, that's all."

He made that huffing noise she'd known so well but had forgotten about. "I wasn't far off when it hit. Coop nearly tossed me, but we made it to your barn."

"And you found me on the ground?"

"I wouldn't have found you at all if not for Chester here." He toed the old dog in the ribs, but it didn't rouse from its fireside nap. "No tellin' how long you would have laid out there, bein' on the offside and all."

She shuddered, the image as cold as she must have been, had she been aware. "I'm grateful, Seth. Truly."

He held her gaze an extra moment before he rose and went to the window. Leaning close, he cupped his hand against the pane. "Foot-high drifts. Sure to grow by morning if it keeps snowing."

She wrapped the quilt around her while his back was turned, then joined him. "I thought we had a least another week. I can't lose all that hay. It's feed for the horses and Ernest—oh!"

She clapped a hand over her mouth.

"Don't worry. They're inside the barn with Coop, bedded down with some of that hay you're so worried about."

His smile warmed her down to her sock-covered toes, and she felt conspicuously ill-dressed.

He must have sensed her discomfort, for he grabbed what looked like one of Pop's shirts from the big chair. "We're both wet as weasels, but there's dry clothes here for you. I'll change upstairs. That'll give you time to, to …" He waved his hand toward her as if he were tossing a ball.

"Pour coffee?"

"Yeah. That."

Darting off like a startled rabbit, he took the stairs two at a time.

CHAPTER 3

Pop Millerton's clothes weren't as big as Seth thought they'd be. In fact, they fit about right. Wet shirt and trousers in hand, he waited at the bedroom doorway until he heard kitchen sounds. Then he eased down the stairs and stepped squarely on a squeaky riser. Dadgum it. His memory wasn't as good as he thought.

"The coast is clear." Abigale trickled her clear-creek laugh he'd always found so remarkable. As if she mimicked the streams that drained off the mountains and into the parks and meadows.

After spreading his clothes out next to Chester and adding more wood to the fire, he took a seat at the kitchen table. "Didn't there used to be more chairs?"

She cut him a sidelong look that said "don't ask," but he already had.

"Well? You chop 'em up for kindling?"

"Funny." She set a mug on the table and filled it with stout coffee. It'd been cooking all this time and could probably float a wagon wheel.

She poured a cup for herself and brought a tin of D.F. Stauffer's crackers to the table. "This will have to do. I haven't baked anything since I arrived."

"When did you get here?"

"Three days ago." She sat in the other chair across the table, took a handful of crackers, and shoved the tin toward him. She never was big on formalities, but he figured that girls' school might have rubbed off some of her charm.

It hadn't.

He chuckled.

"What?"

He fingered through the tin for a lion-shaped cracker and dunked it in his coffee. "I thought you might have changed some after going to that Wolfe Hall up in Denver."

She popped a cracker in her mouth.

"I'm glad to see you haven't."

She wrinkled her nose at him like old times. *Good* times. The tension between them was nearly gone. If only the snow would melt as quickly.

"How long you plan on staying?" He pulled a frown, masking unrealistic hope that she'd never leave.

"Undetermined." Another cookie, followed by a swig of coffee. "Maybe forever."

He coughed and clamped his mouth tight. Had she learned to read minds?

"Does that come as a surprise?"

Coffee flushed the catch in his throat, and he set the cup down gently. "It might to some folks around here."

She stopped with the crackers and gave him her best glare. "What's that supposed to mean?"

"Someone's been cuttin' timber on your land. Since before Pop passed on. I expect he knew." Better she found out from him than someone else, some*place* else. "I've heard rumors it's your neighbor to the south."

"Blackwell." Her face went cold, colorless, and her free hand balled into a fist.

He reached over and covered it with his. Icy. Was she gettin' sick from being wet for so long?

She tried to pull away, but he wouldn't let go. "Abigale."

She looked into her coffee cup.

He squeezed her balled-up hand. "Look at me."

Without raising her head, she glanced up under her brows. Her hair had dried some, and stray curls broke away from her braid and danced around her face, softening her scowl. He wanted to smooth that hair back, but he didn't know exactly what she thought of him. If he was still just a neighboring rancher's gangly son, or if she'd grown feelings like he had for her, missing her something fierce the last two years. Even more so since the funeral.

"Don't go huntin' trouble, Abigale. Let's take care of the barn first, then I'll check at the mills, see where Blackwell's taking the timber. If he's selling it, then we'll get the law involved."

"We?" No invitation in the word. More like a challenge.

Maybe he'd overstepped his bounds. She was seventeen, after all. But she was like family and she was alone. He'd not let her go through all this by herself, even if he had to tie her to that chair.

He squeezed her hand again. "We."

Her fingers relaxed. And her shoulders slumped. Her head dropped lower, and a wet spot hit the table next to her cup.

"If I hadn't left, he might still be alive." Her voice had run back to the little girl who used to pester him.

His chest tightened. "That's not so, and you know it. Pop's time came around, and it would have whether you were here or not. And there's something else you ought to know."

She looked up quick, her brown eyes almost black, shiny with tears.

"You were the best thing that ever happened to him and Mams."

And to me.

⁓

Seth flexed his I'm-older-than-you-muscle—which Abigale highly resented—and made her lie down while he brought in more wood. She'd helped him set the sofa back from the hearth some and covered the worn leather with the log-cabin quilt. He'd spread the other one on the hearth, which was beginning to look like a counter at the dry goods store.

She would have argued more, but her head hurt. Her shoulders and neck hurt. All of her hurt, really. Miraculous that she hadn't broken something when she fell.

And miraculous that Seth Holt just *happened* to be in the area when that crack of lightning hit.

She closed her eyes and her thoughts drifted to Wolfe Hall and back again. She'd not return. Not now. All the main ranch stock had been sold off, but the land was here. The land that Pop and Mams had loved. Her home. She'd not let that Blackwell buzzard get his greedy hands on it by sending one of his hired help to squat on a corner. He'd always had an eye for Pop's timber. Now, with silver mines sprouting and talk of the railroad heading this way, the cry for lumber was even louder. It could be a cash crop for her, along with the hay.

And she'd buy a few head from Seth's family. Start small but start over. Selling out was no longer an option.

The weight of responsibility squeezed a sigh from her chest. How had Pop done it all with only part-time help?

How would she with none?

The door opened and Seth stomped in. Chester's nails clicked across the plank floor as he dashed for his spot by the hearth and shook himself, no doubt scattering snow all over everything drying there.

Abigale was too tired to scold him. Maybe that fall had taken more out of her than she thought. Or maybe she needed real food.

Seth dropped his armload of wood at the end of the hearth and built up the fire. She tracked him to the door, where he hung his slicker on a hook. To the stove, where he poured coffee in a cup, and finally to a spot in front of her, where he dropped to the floor.

The man-smell of him, Pop's pipe smoke in the shirt he wore, his cold breath mixed with coffee—it all made her lonely and she wasn't even alone. She opened her eyes to find him sitting there cross-legged with his hat-flat hair, watching her as if she were a hen's egg about to hatch.

She pushed up on her elbows. "Can you cook?"

"Better than you." He didn't miss a beat or even pretend to.

"I can see you're still as cocky as ever. And speaking of such, the chickens are all gone."

He gave her a wry smirk. "Coyotes, I expect."

"Or weasels."

"Maybe the two-legged variety."

"If someone took the chickens, why wouldn't they take Ernestine?"

"She's more work than chickens. Plus she's a little long in the tooth."

26

Abigale lay back and closed her eyes, the conversation tiring after such a long and brutal day. "Yes, she's old."

"You want some coffee?"

His voice came gentle again, caring. Quite unlike the Seth who always thought he had a better idea.

Slowly shaking her head, she kept her eyes closed for fear she'd see more than she wanted to in his expression. He sat too close. Not that she didn't trust him. She didn't trust her own emotions now that she was alone in the world for the second time.

Danger lay in that line of thinking. She hadn't had a good cry since the funeral, and she didn't want to start now. "Tomorrow I'll ride in and pick up supplies. I have a little money and I know where Pop kept his stash."

Silence answered.

She peeked.

Seth's arms propped on his knees, his eyes closed, the coffee cup dangling from one hand and about to fall.

She took hold of the cup and eased it from his fingers. If she were twelve, she'd push him over.

But she wasn't twelve, and he'd given her nothing but hard work, loyalty, and kindness.

She set the cup on the floor and brushed his arm with her fingertips. "Seth."

He jerked awake and blinked at her, as if trying to get his bearings. "I always wondered what it'd be like waking up next to you."

His face flushed red again and he pushed from the floor with a grumble. "Never mind that. I'm just tired." Rubbing the back of his neck, he looked around. For what, she didn't know. "I'm, uh, I'm gonna sleep by the fire if that's all right with you. Snow's piling up and you'll need more wood soon."

He offered his hand. "I can help you upstairs."

Her hackles rose at his assumption that she needed help, but she was too weary to argue. Besides, he shouldn't be pushing Coop through several miles of drifts in the middle of the night.

She tugged the quilt under her chin and slid further into the cushions. "That's fine with me. Sleep where you will, but I'm staying right here. And you'd better not snore."

~

Drip-drip-drip staccatoed into Abigale's dreams like her piano teacher's insistence that she practice-practice-practice. Waking, she turned her head toward the window, where blue sky and sunshine accompanied the musical melting of snow.

She pushed upright and questioned her memory. Had she only fallen off her crude ladder or been run over by stampeding cattle as well?

Wincing with the effort, she swung her feet to the floor, comforted once more by the thick wool socks that covered them.

And where was Seth? The last she'd seen him, he was stretched out on Mams's braided rug in front of the hearth. Snoring.

Coffee's tempting aroma lured her to the stove, where she found a not-so-tempting can of beans and a towel-covered pan of—flatbread? She shoved aside her irritation and bit into a palm-sized round.

Not a bad effort for having no milk or baking powder.

So he could cook. She could rope, ride, and shoot. Not that those skills had earned her any points at Wolfe Hall.

After a second round and a cup of strong coffee, she managed to make it upstairs to her room, where she met a horrible sight in her dressing-table mirror.

"Pop would say I look like I'd been rode hard and put up wet." She sat on the small bench and unbraided her hair. "He'd be half right. Fallen hard and carried in wet."

Carefully she combed out the tangles, wincing at a knot on the back of her head and a little dried blood. Seth had tended to more than her feet, and her insides warmed at the thought.

She fetched a pitcher of water from downstairs for her basin and washed her face and hands. Movement outside her bedroom window caught her eye, and she paused to watch Seth scale the side of the barn, finishing the ladder she'd started, but using what looked like bigger pieces of wood. Pride in her idea warred with gratitude that he'd taken on the task himself.

Making herself more presentable—though not on Seth's account—she tied her hair back with a ribbon and went outside feeling a little better.

The snow was nearly gone from level ground, other than drifts that hugged the buildings, but not from the white-mantled summit rising east of the ranch like a watchful giant. Winter was settling in. She hugged her waist and hunched her shoulders. It'd be a lonely Christmas this year without Pop. *Godey's* magazine mentioned nothing about celebrating by oneself.

She'd planned to come home for the holidays, so she was only a couple of weeks early. A couple of weeks and a bundle of heartache. If she'd known how ill he was, she would have gladly left her classes behind.

"Good morning."

At the greeting from atop the barn, she looked up to see a scruffy face grinning down. "Or should I say good afternoon?"

She grabbed a handful of drifted snow, quickly formed a ball, and lobbed it.

CHAPTER 4

S eth ducked and laughed. "You couldn't hit the broad side of a barn."

Another snowball cut closer.

"Or the roof either."

"You're taking a mighty big risk, Seth Holt, giving me lip from up there. I can knock these slats out as easily as you nailed them in."

He wouldn't put it past her. She always had gotten her back up when he teased her.

He pulled his neckerchief off and waved it in the air.

She hit it with a snowball.

"Hey, that was a flag of truce."

"No, it wasn't. It was your old, grimy neckerchief you got for Christmas one year."

She was right, and he was somehow pleased that she remembered the details.

He peeked over the edge. She was standing with her hands on her hips looking just about as pretty as he'd ever seen her. *Shoot.*

"I'm coming down, and if you take any potshots, I'll rub your face in the snow."

She laughed.

Maybe if he threatened to kiss her, that would hold her at bay.

Whoa, cowboy.

He shoved the hammer in his belt and started his descent on slats deliberately set to accommodate his stride and not Abigale's. The thought of her climbing up the side of the barn when he wasn't here turned his stomach.

At the last slat, several feet off the ground, he jumped.

"You spaced them too far apart." A scowl bunched her pretty brows, and she nailed him with a squinty-eyed stare. "You did that on purpose."

Nearly impossible not to laugh at her, he answered with a frown of his own. "So what if I did? You don't need to be shimmying up the side of the barn and fall off again."

She stepped in closer and tipped her head back, glaring up at him. "And you don't need to be telling me what I can and cannot do on my own place."

He smelled coffee on her breath. She'd never looked more kissable. And he'd never been so distracted by such a singular impossibility.

He picked up the leftover slats and took them to Pop's workroom before she got it in her head to start nailing them in between those he'd set.

She dogged him into the barn like Chester, and since she wouldn't accept his peace offering, he threw her a bone instead. "If you can rig something so I can haul up this pile of shingles, I'll start on the roof."

That set her mind to working. He could almost hear the gears grinding as she spun around and stalked out of the barn.

Ernestine watched him and offered her opinion over the stall gate as she chewed her cud. Thankfully he didn't have to milk her, but that wasn't necessarily good news. A dry cow meant no milk, cream, or butter. His folks always had extra, and they'd share. Or he could bring over one of their cows until Ernestine was bred come spring.

Chester watched him too, and Seth was surprised the dog hadn't followed Abigale inside.

"I need to tell my folks where I am."

The dog whined.

"You're right. I can't leave before the roof is finished or she'll be up there doin' it herself. And if she freezes up like she did on the waterfall, she won't be able to climb down."

The dog shook its head as if remembering that incident so long ago.

Seth did, and it was as clear in his mind as if it were yesterday. "I'm not doing *that* again."

While he waited for Abigale, Seth let the horses and cow out, and they hoofed it to the south pasture. What snow hadn't blown away was fast melting into the arms of a sunny day. A streak of sunshine would give him time to check on Blackwell's timber pilfering, get Abigale settled in, and build up her woodpile.

It'd sure be a lot easier if she'd go home with him. His ma and pa would welcome her. So would his little sister, Emmy. In fact, she'd be tickled.

And he had more hope of gettin' milk out of Chester than convincing Abigale to come to the Lazy H for the winter.

His stomach rumbled, and he thought of the flat bread and beans he'd fixed that morning. He needed something more substantial than coffee if he was gonna get anything done, so he set out for the house and a second breakfast.

At the porch he stomped off his boots, then entered to the hum of a treadle sewing machine.

"Take your boots off," Abigale ordered without looking up.

"You think I don't know that?" Wedging a boot heel in the beetle-like jaws of a jack under the coat rack, he yanked one off, then the other, and dropped his hat on a hook.

He'd rather say other things to her, but she was making it hard not to squabble, which meant she still saw him as a schoolboy. Which irritated him all the more, confounded woman.

"You leave me anything to eat?"

She cut him a sideways look. "Where'd you learn to make flat bread? It wasn't half bad."

"That's a back-handed complement if I ever heard one."

"I imagine you don't hear enough to know the difference, do you?"

At that she giggled. Real pleased with herself, she was.

More than half a pan remained, and he took most of it and reached for his boots.

"Wait." She approached with a quilted sack in her hands. "Please." Her expression softened. "I want to show you this, and if you'll wait, I'll get some preserves for that bread." Pulling out a table chair, she laid the sack in front of it. Then she took two plates from a cupboard, added a couple of knives and spoons from a drawer, and refilled last night's mugs with hot coffee.

In a different cupboard she found a tarnished sugar bowl and a dish of red preserves.

Strawberry, he hoped.

She took the other chair. "You didn't look very far if you searched the cupboards."

A smile softened what sounded like criticism, so he chose it over her words. "I found what I needed."

She sugared her coffee and pushed the preserves toward him. "How empty was the flour bin?"

"Pretty near. Same with the lard. Plenty of salt, sugar, and coffee, though."

"That sounds about right. I think Pop could live on coffee alone." She stirred hers but didn't offer him the sugar bowl. "If I recall, you drink yours strong and black."

That made two things about him she remembered. "Yes, ma'am." He lifted the cup to his lips and winked at her. An old habit.

She flustered a little and glanced down at her plate. Spittin' nails at him one minute and blushing the next. As changeable as the summit in spring.

He picked up the sack she'd made from an old quilt and checked the strength of the stitches where a long strap attached. Looping it over his head and one shoulder, he tugged hard, then laid it back on the table. "This'll work just fine. Thank you."

"If you run a rope through your belt and over the edge of the barn, you can send the sack down empty, I'll fill it with shingles for you, then you can pull it back up to the roof."

"You won't try yankin' me off the barn?"

She spread a spoonful of preserves on a piece of bread and bit into it with a saucy look his way.

He'd give his saddle to know what she was really thinking rather than whatever was going to pop out of her mouth after she swallowed. Those eyes turned him inside out.

Wiping the corners of her mouth with her thumb and finger didn't help either. "That depends."

Leaving her alone wasn't going to be easy, but Pop and Mams weren't around. He'd best finish up with the roof and woodpile as soon as possible and beat a trail back to his folks' place.

~

Just when Abigale thought things were more grownup between them, Seth had to go and make some harebrained remark that made her feel like she was ten. Well, if that was what he wanted, she'd give it to him. But it wasn't what she wanted anymore. Theirs was a tricky relationship. Safe when they were kids—in spite of his teasing—and shaky now that it was only the two of them, with him a full-grown man trying to do for her. And looking better than anything she'd seen wearing trousers in Denver.

He'd cuffed his sleeves back, and his bare forearms rested on the table. Not exactly the best of manners, but the show of such harnessed strength made her feel safe, somehow. Protected.

Two days' growth on his jawline accentuated his mossy-green eyes that drew her in like their secret swimming hole used to. But she couldn't allow loneliness and memories to influence her actions or cloud her thinking. She had to let Seth Holt know she could stand on her own two legs.

Even if her world had turned upside down.

"Depends on what?"

His words cut through her wool-gathering.

She ignored his full-mouth speech for the moment. "On whether you need me to show you how to lay shingles."

He nearly choked.

She shoved the jar across the table. "Here. It won't be so dry with these strawberry preserves."

He was getting harder to read. What looked like the old teasing Seth could flash in a heartbeat to something she didn't recognize. Something in that full-grown man that reminded her she *wasn't* ten. Something she wanted to keep here with her.

He'd better go as soon as possible.

"If we haul up several loads of shingles, I can ride into Divide for supplies while you're nailing them down. But first I'm going to check the root cellar. Pop was good about laying things by."

"I'm going with you."

She stared at him, her breath cutting sharp against her ribs. "To the root cellar?"

"To town."

He was impossible.

She let out a tight breath and took her plate to the sink. "That'll cost you another day here. I can go to town by myself. I'm a grown wo—"

"Yes, ma'am, you are. That's why I'm going with you."

He put his plate in the sink on top of hers, downed his coffee, and set the preserves next to the sugar bowl, centered on the table like two peas in a pod. "I'll take a load of shingles up while you're checking the cellar."

With that, he pulled his boots on, grabbed his hat, and left.

She stood in the kitchen debating whether she should yell out the door at him or stomp her foot. Instead she picked up a basket and headed to the cellar.

If viewed from across the pasture, the small grassy mound didn't draw the eye but blended with the natural rise and fall in the land that bunched up at the base of the mountain. But the path from the house that wound past the necessary and into an aspen grove led to the stone-faced side of the mound and the wooden door of Pop and Mams's root cellar.

Abigale stopped in front of the trees, the ache of missing her adoptive grandparents nearly bending her in half. They had truly rescued her, saved her from an orphanage or worse when they'd brought her to their ranch. Dim memories of her parents hung like a thin curtain at the back of her mind, but she'd long ago lost their faces. All that remained was a vague sense of safety that had been suddenly and swiftly torn away.

Pop and Mams had filled her life since, and if she was certain of anything, it was their love for her.

That was why she'd agreed to go to Wolfe Hall. They'd been so proud to send her and had gladly set aside money that could have been used elsewhere. But Abigale began to lose heart when Mams died the first year, and with Pop's passing …

Well, it was too much. She belonged here, on the land they loved. The land she loved.

Instinctively her head turned toward the aspens, their bare white limbs a skeletal contrast to the dark fir and pine. The forest stood in sentinel posture hedging the house and barn, perfuming the air with its woodsy scent.

Ahead, the root cellar waited as she remembered it—a frighteningly dark place in her childhood that, over the years, became a treasured repository of root vegetables, salted meat, even rounds and squares of butter. She'd not thought to bring the lantern, so she propped the door open with a large rock set aside for that purpose.

As expected, the cellar's treasures had been plundered in the two years since Mams's passing. But Pop had laid in potatoes, carrots, squash, and salt pork, though no butter or fresh preserves. A few jars of peaches remained.

She filled her basket, shut the door securely, and headed down the path toward the house. A rhythmic *tap-tap-pause*, *tap-tap-pause* sounded through the clear air, and from her slightly higher position she saw Seth on the barn roof, kneeling on one knee, her quilt-bag slung around him.

The same descriptors that had come to mind yesterday returned as she watched him. *Hardworking, loyal, kind.* All three defined the man she'd known most of her life. But so did handsome, strong, and appealing.

She shook her head, scattering such thoughts, and took her basket to the house, where she put everything in its place and hurried upstairs to change and fix her hair. It'd take her no time to hitch up the mare.

No time at all. For when she stepped outside, the mare, wagon, and Seth were waiting at the end of the path leading from the front door. Seth took up more than half the seat, reins in hand like they were about to go for a Sunday drive.

CHAPTER 5

I f Abigale Millerton kept stealing his breath every time Seth looked at her, he'd have no breath at all by the time they got to town.

She'd changed her britches and boots for the fancy dress upstairs, and he thought he knew where she'd put that funny contraption he'd seen on the chair in her room. She'd also piled her hair under the little hat and looked like something out of a magazine he'd once seen his ma reading.

He was still wearing Pop Millerton's clothes and hadn't shaved in a week.

Abigale accepted his offered hand and climbed to the seat.

His tongue wrapped around his eye teeth and he couldn't see what he wanted to say about how she looked. And smelled. She'd done something that shoved hay and horsehair to the background and brought spring flowers to mind.

Lord, have mercy on his cowboy heart.

He flicked the reins and the mare started out.

"Thanks for hitching up Tess." She smoothed her skirt over the high-topped shoes, and their pointed toes peeked out under the edge. "How'd you know she was the one?"

Well, maybe that's because I recognized Pop's two broken-down saddle horses and Ernestine doesn't hitch well to a wagon.

Hardest thing in all the world was keeping those words to himself. Temptation always hooked him by the jaw, and words got him in more trouble than whiskey or cards ever could.

"You not talking to me?" She looked over at him with her big brown eyes, double daring him to speak his mind.

"No, ma'am."

"You've said that more than once. Since when am I a ma'am? I'm as unmarried as Ernestine, and you've known me nearly all my life. What's wrong, cat got your tongue?"

"You're looking mighty fine this morning."

She patted the back of her hair and glanced away from him, like she was checking the pastures. "Thank you."

If she dressed like that in Denver, why *wasn't* she married? Or didn't those gals see many menfolk at that fancy school?

And what would someone as fine as Abigale Millerton ever see in him?

Rancher's son and cow puncher.

Eighth-grade graduate.

Repairer of barn roofs and splitter of firewood.

She let out a sigh. "I'd forgotten how beautiful it is up here. So *clean*. Not at all like Denver."

He looked around too, taking in the grassland and the way the timber and aspens trickled down from the slopes and creeped in at the edges. "It's easy to take for granted what we're used to seeing."

"Why, Seth Holt." Her gaze swept him with something near to admiration. "I do believe there's a poet hiding somewhere inside you." The corners of her mouth bowed up.

She was mocking him.

Liable to say something fight-worthy any minute, he slapped Tess into a brisk trot. He and Abigale had ridden horseback all over this valley, up into the timber, and over the lower slopes. They'd fished and tracked deer, trailed maverick steers, and found the waterfall. But he'd never sat beside her like this, isolated right out in the open together.

"Where'd you get this wagon?"

She fussed with a little bag on her wrist and scooted back more on the seat. Her right leg, flush against his left one, warmed that side of his body and all of his brain.

"I made arrangements with Pastor Meeks when I was here for the funeral. He said I could borrow it as long as I needed. Tess too."

So she'd planned to come back. The thought stoked a slow-burning fire inside him.

As they rode into town, a few folks stopped and watched them pass, probably wondering what he was doing with such a fine-looking woman on such a muddy morning.

He stopped in front of the mercantile and helped her down to the boardwalk. "You sure you don't need money?"

She puffed out a little sound that meant he'd wasted his time. "No, thank you."

Like an afterthought, she hesitated and searched his face, hunting something important. "But it was kind of you to ask."

Whoa.

He reset his hat and glanced at the storefront. "While you're inside, I'll ask around about Blackwell and where he mills his timber."

With a gloved hand she touched his arm, her fingers warm and firm. "Be careful. Don't start anything."

He covered her hand with his and gave it a little squeeze. "Don't worry about me. I can take care of myself. I'm a grown—"

"Yes, you are." She nailed him with a pointed look. "That's why I said what I did."

Now that was the pot talkin' to the kettle.

She lifted her chin and headed into the store, leaving him watching her like an orphaned pup.

Bootsteps sounded behind him. "Mornin' Seth."

He turned to Hoot Spicer's rowdy grin. A grin Seth would just as soon wipe off the man's bushy face, but he thumbed his waistband instead. "Mornin', Hoot. Business been good?"

The old man stroked his whiskers, sharp eyes gleaming. He owned one of the biggest mills around and just might know the answer to Seth's most pressing question.

However, Seth started with another one. "Café still serving?"

Henry "Hoot" Spicer was wealthier than anyone else in town, but he liked to eat and never turned down a free meal.

"I do believe they are." He slapped Seth's shoulder. "Haven't seen you in a while, son. Your folks doin' well?"

Before Seth could answer, he continued, "How 'bout you buy me a cup o' coffee and we swap lies."

Seth relinquished a full-blown laugh. "Suits me right down to the ground."

If only he could read Abigale as easily as he read Hoot Spicer.

~

"Morning, Miss Abigale. I didn't expect to see you again quite so soon." Thomas Briggs pushed his spectacles to the bridge of his nose and dipped his head politely. "Sorry about your grandfather."

"Thank you, Mr. Briggs." Abigale drank in the familiar mix of leather goods and soap, tobacco and wood smoke. Nothing in Denver had ever smelled as welcoming as Briggs' Mercantile and Dry Goods, in spite of her attendant grief.

"I'm out of nearly everything at the ranch, and after last night's storm, I fear we may be in for a hard winter."

His spectacles had slipped again, and he regarded her over their rims. "You staying on?"

She bristled against the ill-concealed worry in his voice.

"Is there a reason I should not?"

"Well, uh …" He glanced out the window and tugged at his bibbed apron. "No, I suppose not. But it is a ways out to your place and, uh, there's been a lot of activity at the mills lately."

She left the cracker barrel and faced him across the counter. "Just spit it out, Mr. Briggs." Miss Butterfield would suffer the vapors at such a brash remark, but Abigale's days of proper deportment were behind her. Now it was about surviving.

The man returned his spectacles to their intended perch and cleared his throat. "Not that I know anything for certain,"—he glanced out the window again—"but I've *heard* that some fine timber has been running through the Windsor Mill. Lodgepole. Like grows up at the base of the mountain."

Around here, everyone knew her grandfather's land skirted the north face of Pikes Peak where a thick patch of lodgepole pine grew. Between that stand and the rich grassland, it was a coveted area.

She pushed at the back of her hat and flinched, forgetful of the knot on her head. "I'll take two fifty-pound bags of flour, ten pounds of sugar, twenty of Arbuckles', butter if you have it, and whatever canned or dried fruit is available."

Surely Seth's parents had some beef they'd sell her. "A can of baking powder, if you have any." She leaned to the right, eyeing the shelf behind the storekeeper. "I also need some cinnamon and nutmeg. And do you have confectioners' sugar? The fine, powdery kind?"

Mr. Briggs blinked a couple of times.

"Do you have these things?"

"Yes, Miss Abigale, I do." He cleared his throat and relocated his spectacles once more.

She was tempted to suggest he tie a string from one side of the eyeglasses to the other and loop it around his head. "I have the cash, if that's what you're worried about."

His shoulders relaxed.

So that was it. He expected her to ask for credit.

"Excuse me, Mr. Briggs, but if I did not have the money, would that have been a problem, considering my grandfather's pristine reputation where credit was concerned?"

The storekeeper stooped behind the counter and retrieved a crate for her purchases, planting it between them as if to shield himself from her questioning.

She shoved it aside and leaned slightly forward. "How long have you known us, Thomas?"

His brows creased at her use of his given name, and he turned to the shelving behind him. "Several years, miss."

In all those years, she'd never seen Thomas Briggs so jittery. "What are you not telling me?"

He began filling the crate, rather hurriedly. "Things have changed in the two years you haven't been here regular."

Dread slid up her back and snaked along her neck. "In what way?"

"Land is at a premium. Especially timbered land. With the railroad coming this way and glory holes pocking the countryside, sawmills are barely keeping pace with demand. Some ranchers are eyeing neighboring land and putting pressure on folks to sell. Them that aren't doing so already, like yourself."

Little beads of sweat appeared on the man's forehead, and he mopped them with his apron. "And some are just cutting the trees without buying. Mind you, I've just *heard* such talk."

Abigale gripped the counter's edge for balance, the back of her head throbbing like a drum. Based on Thomas Briggs' demeanor, *putting pressure on* was his cautious substitution for *threatening*.

"And is some of that pressure applied to merchants offering credit to said landowners?"

He dabbed his forehead again.

Opening her reticule, she was distracted by a folded square of silky green displayed in the glass-topped case and thought at once of Seth. She hesitated only a moment before withdrawing enough money to pay for her supplies.

With eyes on the silk and voice lowered to a hush, she tucked Mr. Briggs' receipt in her bag. "We did not have this conversation, sir, and you have told me nothing."

She glanced up with a final whisper. "But I thank you."

CHAPTER 6

Abigale saw so much red, she had a hard time seeing Seth leaning against the wagon until he moved.

"You get what you needed?"

Ignoring his question and hand, she hiked her skirt and climbed to the seat. "It's inside."

He made some predictably male sound in his throat, but she was spit-fire mad at men at the moment, and since he was the closest one within firing range, the less she said to him, the better.

The bell above Briggs' door jangled as he entered, and again when he came out with a flour sack over each shoulder. The wagon shuddered as they landed in the bed. If he busted those bags open, he'd pay her every red cent of the outrageous five dollars it cost her.

And what will you pay him for bringing you in from the snow and fixing the barn roof?

The ramrod in her spine weakened, and she fingered the tender spot on the back of her head. Seth Holt was not the enemy. In fact, he'd probably saved her life. The least she could do was be cordial. Grateful wouldn't hurt either.

She stared straight ahead when the bell jangled again. A jolt and the scrape of wood on wood announced the crate. Another hundred pounds of supplies.

Guilt wiggled in around her collar for buying confectioners' sugar, paying twice as much for it as she would have in Denver. But what would Christmas be without iced cookies and cake?

What would Christmas be without Pop?

The wagon tipped as Seth climbed to the seat. Silent and simmering, he unwrapped the reins from the brake handle and snapped them against Tess's rump.

Abigale focused on loosening her stranglehold on her reticule. "I need to stop at the land office as well."

Without a word, nod, or glance, he reined in at the end of the street.

"I'll only be a moment." Most unladylike, she clambered down, completely unconcerned with the thoughts of anyone who was rude enough to be watching. But she was as good as her word on the time it took her to clear Millerton land from the sale ledger. Paid off long before she'd come to there, it had no liens and nothing to prevent her from keeping it. So long as she could pay the taxes the following year.

She'd think about that later.

Seth was still brooding, and she couldn't very well blame him. However, pride clogged her throat and they drove five miles out of town before she'd calmed herself enough to open her mouth without yelling. Or crying.

"Thank you for your help."

Silence.

"You have been nothing but kind and thoughtful."

From the corner of her eye, she saw him turn and look at her, but she couldn't meet his gaze. Not yet.

Listen quick and speak slow, Pop had always said. *Get mad even slower.*

She'd not done so well on that last account. But how else was she supposed to feel after learning that someone really was stealing her timber? Thomas Briggs had fairly said so outright.

Time to eat crow, and to her way of thinking, the feathers were the hardest part.

"I'm sorry I snapped at you in town, but you're a man, and—"

Seth huffed. "You noticed."

She might not survive the trip home. "Seth Leopold Holt, you're making it awfully hard to be nice after what I learned at Briggs's Mercantile."

"And what was that, Abigale Rebecca Millerton?"

One of them had to stop the war of words. It might as well be her. "Someone really is cutting timber on Pop's land. And they're *pressuring* merchants to not extend credit to certain landowners in the area."

Seth's silence bothered her as much as his quick comebacks, and she studied him boldly, trying to read what was firing around behind his hazel eyes.

He shot a glance her way. "Why did you say *pressuring* like you did?"

"Because that was the word Thomas Briggs used and I interpreted it as *threatening*. Of course, I implied that I wouldn't share anything he told me but telling you doesn't count."

"What's that supposed to mean?" Seth's tone carried an edge she didn't like, but she was determined not to fight with him.

"It means I trust you. You're all I've got."

"In spite of my being of the male persuasion?"

She sagged at her choice of words.

"Why do you lump me in with all *men*? Especially when you say it like every man is a scoundrel that has hurt you in some way?"

He stopped Tess right in the middle of the trail and faced Abigale straight on.

She expected an all-out yelling match, but he lowered his voice and his eyes went dark as a pine forest. "Did someone in Denver hurt you, Abigale? If he did, he'll regret it at my hand, I swear."

Stunned by the intensity of his expression and voice, she touched his arm. "No, Seth. No one has hurt me, not like that."

"Like what, then?"

She pressed both hands to her temples, willing her emotions to settle, to not boil over like an unwatched pot. "I keep meeting with opposition, and it's getting the better of me."

"Did you have trouble at the land office?"

"No."

"Was Briggs difficult?"

"No." She shook her head. "If anything, he was helpful. I'm sorry. I don't know what else to say."

Seth studied the countryside, rubbing one thumb back and forth on the leather reins before tapping Tess. The mare jerked ahead. "I'd say you're missing Pop and trying to carry the burden of the ranch all by yourself."

"What I mean is—"

"I know what you mean." The look he gave her softened to match the change in his tone. "Neither one of us does very well at saying what we mean, but I understand."

His eyes held her, longer than before. She couldn't look away and noticed they'd changed to meadow-green with flecks of gold. As if they contained the whole high-country range within them, from summer to fall.

Tess stumbled, and her misstep broke the moment as Seth looked back to the trail.

Abigale did the same, but something had shifted inside her. Something small and warm like a candle flame in the dark that she didn't want to extinguish.

"Did Briggs mention any names of who was doing the so-called pressuring?"

She kept her eyes ahead, watching the light change on the summit as clouds gathered around it. A massive hen with her chicks scuttling in for another storm. "No, he didn't."

Only then did she remember that Seth had set out to gather information in town. "Did you learn anything from anyone?"

She looked in time to see his jaw tighten—an old sign from childhood that warned of an impending storm as clearly as clouds gathering around the snowy peak.

~

Seth ground his back teeth, biting down words sure to kindle a grass fire if he let them. Abigale had run him into the same corral as every other man, and he resented it in spite of telling her he understood. It'd be nice not to have to understand, to hear straight out that she respected him for who he was.

Though she had admitted that she trusted him. That was something.

"Hoot Spicer gave me an earful."

She waited four hoofbeats before leaning over and looking straight at him like she used to when he ignored her. "Well?"

Dadgum it, she'd make him loco yet.

"He didn't come right out and say Blackwell, but he came so close, I could hear him thinkin' it. I was hoping Briggs had mentioned the name, so we'd have something solid to go on."

Tess clomped on for another half-mile, and Abigale sat uncharacteristically silent.

"What are you thinking?"

She cut him a silent glance that could stampede an entire herd.

"Whatever it is, it sounds like a bad idea."

She unpinned her hat and took it off, heedless of the sun that made her yellow hair nearly white. "How can you say that? You haven't heard it yet."

"No, but I see it on your face, and it looks like trouble. You need to let me handle this, man to man."

She slapped his shoulder with her hat.

He nearly laughed but—thank the Lord—he didn't. He wasn't a complete idiot. "What was that for?"

"What makes you think *I* can't handle things? Just because I'm a woman, you act like I can't think or do anything for myself."

"I do not." But he was thinking it. Thinking how she'd get herself in a jackpot. Abigale Millerton was smart and capable enough to do whatever she set her mind to, and that was what scared him. Blackwell was no one to mess with, and every *man* in the county knew it.

"Tell me, then." A sudden image of his ma pushed the next word through his lips. "Please."

"Promise you won't try to stop me?"

"No."

She folded her arms with a hard *humph*. "Then I'll just keep it to myself."

"And I'll hide your saddles and tack, and camp out in your barn until the snow's so deep you can't get anywhere on foot."

A warning shot fired from her eyes. "You wouldn't."

"Try me."

Another mile, and the Millerton barn came into view. He ought to cut across country to his folks' place, let them know what was going on, and get his ma and sister to work on Abigale until she agreed to stay there. Then he could deal with Blackwell himself.

Best plan he'd heard all day.

He turned Tess off the trail and out over the grassy park that stretched uncluttered until it reached the buildings of the Lazy H, mere specs in the distance.

The wagon bucked over rough ground, and Abigale held to the edge of the bench seat with both hands. "Seth Holt, what are you doing?"

"I'm taking you home."

"You'll do no such thing. Turn around right this minute. I paid for a wagon load of stores that I intend to make last me through the winter. And this is my wagon and mare for as long as I need them."

His ploy was successful. Worry curled the edge of her voice.

"I'll turn around when you tell me what you've got cooking in that pretty little head of yours."

That last part was probably a mistake. She'd consider it condescending and might stab him with that vicious-looking hat pin. But what was he supposed to do with a headstrong gal liable to get herself in a fix worse than the one he'd already pulled her out of?

She crossed her arms again but fell against him when they rolled over a badger hole. Quick as a whip, he looped an arm around her and held her close.

"Let me go." She pushed against his ribs.

"Not until you tell me what you're planning. Besides, if you bounce out, I'll have to stop and fetch you, and we might not make the ranch before the storm hits."

She looked over her shoulder toward the mountain, her face so close that all he had to do was turn his head and kiss her. The temptation was almost more than he could handle. She smelled even better close up, and he knew right then and there his bachelor days were running out on him. He had to marry Abigale Millerton.

But first he had to win her over.

She went soft against him. "All right."

"All right what?"

"All right, I'll tell you."

Reluctantly, he let her go, and she sat up straighter. She didn't have room to scoot away, but at least she hadn't tried. A good sign.

"I'm going to hide out in the woods where Blackwell— or whomever—has been cutting and wait for him to show up with his crew."

A bad sign.

A very bad sign.

But he needed to hear her *whole* plan, and if he jumped in the middle of it too early, she'd sull up and not tell him. "Go on."

She raised her hope-filled face toward him. "You think it will work?"

"Is there more to it?"

"Well,"—she pushed at the knot of hair that was bouncing loose—"I've always been a good shot."

CHAPTER 7

Seth hauled back on the reins so hard, Abigale lurched forward but caught herself on the buckboard before she tumbled onto Tess.

The look on his face made her want to jump down and walk home. It wasn't all that far, though the trek would ruin her shoes. But she needed the supplies in the wagon, and didn't put it past him to drive off with them.

Gathering the last vestiges of her pride, she adjusted her seating and tugged on her suit jacket. "I wouldn't kill him, if that's what you're worried about."

Seth took his hat off with a groan and rubbed his forehead before slapping the hat back on. She'd never seen him quite so pale, and it made his stubbly beard even darker. The man was entirely too handsome for her own good. Heavens, if the girls at Wolfe Hall saw him now, they'd be setting their caps and flirting up a storm.

The revelation did not settle well. He was *her* Seth. *Her* friend. She glanced at the mountain again, amazed once more at how fast a squall could gather in this high country.

The memory of their fireside evening came flooding back. The comfort of his presence. The camaraderie they'd shared, so like their days growing up together. Of course they'd squabbled as children too, but it seemed more intense now. Why was he so set against her establishing herself as a viable landowner in this valley? Why couldn't he support her rather than oppose her every move?

She resigned herself to a tirade. The sooner he blew off steam, the sooner they could get home and unload the supplies.

"Go ahead, get it over with. Tell me all the reasons you think my idea is foolish and why you have a better one, and then turn around so we can make it to the ranch before the storm hits."

A sudden gust whipped past them, snagging the remains of her updo and lashing it across her face. She gathered her hair in one hand and twisted it over her shoulder.

Seth clucked Tess back around the way they had come, and by the time they made the trail, the sun was buried in a growing cloud bank. Abigale shivered.

With one arm, he drew her close against him, quickening the mare's pace with his other hand. Still, he hadn't said a word.

All Abigale could read from his stoic profile was determination to reach shelter. But the strength of his arm around her and the warmth of his body added a dimension she'd not appreciated earlier. Never, in fact. She'd not been aware of him carrying her inside the house, and as a young girl, she'd always taken for granted—and resented—the fact that he was physically stronger.

But now, in a race against nature, she was grateful for their differences. And grateful he was with her.

The sky dropped, belching snow in fits and spurts. Seth reined up in front of the house and climbed over the back of the seat to the wagon bed.

Abigale hurried to the porch where she propped the front door open in spite of the rising wind. He brought the flour in first, setting both sacks against the kitchen wall, and returned moments later with the crate. She cleared the table of cloth, sugar bowl, and preserves in time for him to set the crate there. Then he was out the door, closing it hard behind him.

Through the window she watched him pull his hat down and drive the wagon inside the barn. He did it all without being asked, as if it were his place to do so, unprotected though he was without his slicker or canvas coat.

Why such sacrifice on his part? Did he consider it his Christian duty, or was this his version of support?

He certainly wasn't opposing her now.

She hung her jacket over a chair back and unpacked the crate, stacking canned goods in the cupboards, setting the lard and butter in covered crockery, Arbuckles' near the grinder. After stoking the cookstove, she put on a pot of coffee, then went to the fireplace, where she poked around in the ashes for signs of life.

One coal winked up at her hungrily, and she fed it broken bits of kindling, adding larger pieces until a small but steady flame maintained itself between the andirons. Finally, she added several split logs—thanks to Seth's efforts with the axe, though she could have done the same. She'd split firewood countless times and expected to do so indefinitely. After all, she would be living alone.

Sobered by the reality of her predicament, she glanced at Pop's shotgun and Henry rifle above the mantel. Her idea of taking potshots at the timber thieves didn't seem quite so clever now with snow swirling around the house. What had she been thinking?

A log caught flame and snapped into her musing. Seth would be hungry and so was she. A canned-peach pie seemed a good match for coffee. And with the side pork and potatoes she'd brought in from the cellar, she'd have a solid meal cooking in no time.

She'd not prepared supper in ages, not since she'd been home last summer, helping Pop with the haying. Since she couldn't heft a fifty-pound bag of flour into the storage bin by herself, she scooped out what she'd need for two pies, cut lard into the bowl, and added salt and water. In no time, rolled-out dough draped two pie plates with strips left over for the top. She poured in two tins of peaches, topped them with a mix of sugar, cinnamon, and a little flour, and crossed strips across each pie like lattice work. After trimming and crimping off the edges, both pans went in the oven.

With a heady sense of accomplishment, she caught her reflection in the darkened window—untidy, windblown, and flour-dusted.

Boots stomped on the porch, and she fled up the stairs. She couldn't let Seth see her looking so—so *wild*!

~

Coffee and cinnamon hit Seth in the face as soon as he opened the door. He hadn't eaten much in town with Hoot Spicer, and it merely primed the pump. He pulled his boots off and pegged his hat, then socked over to the stove and lifted the lid on a large skillet. Potatoes, side pork, onions.

He'd died and gone to heaven after all.

Another scent tickled his innards, and he peeked inside the oven. Peach pie. Lord, have mercy.

He poured himself a cup of coffee and looked around for Abigale, but she must have gone upstairs. A log shifted in the fireplace, sending sparks up the chimney, and the big chair invited him to rest a while. He eased into it and stretched his feet out on the hearth stones.

If this was what it felt like to have a home and a wife of his own, then sign him up. 'Cept Pop Millerton's place wasn't his and neither was Pop's stubborn, independent-minded granddaughter.

Why couldn't Abigale be one of those easygoing, domesticated gals who only cooked up meals, not wild-hare schemes for lying wait on snakes who had no qualms about stealing from a woman?

Whoever the varmint was, he'd picked the wrong woman. And if Abigale Millerton *was* some namby-pamby gal, Seth wouldn't be sitting in her house itching to follow-through with her harebrained plan and wishing she were his wife.

"Comfortable?"

He jerked his feet back and spilled hot coffee on his leg.

She came around the end of the sofa, where she settled and tucked her feet under a simpler dress than what she'd worn to town. Her braid hung over her shoulder. Prettier than a picture, she was. He rubbed a hand along his whiskered jaw and clamped his elbows close to his sides in case he was getting ripe.

What he wouldn't give for a shave and a bath.

"You haven't told me what you thought of my plan."

The sofa was still facing the hearth, but he angled his chair back some so he could see her without being so obvious about it.

She picked up the pillow he'd propped her head on last night and traced the fancy needlework.

He had a hard time picturing her sitting still long enough to make something like that. "How's your head?"

She slid him a look. "I asked first."

There was no sneaking up on Abigale Millerton, a fact for sure. Technically, she hadn't asked him a question, but he let it slide. "I've given it some thought."

Hopefulness showed up again. "Really?"

"Tell me more about it. Other than how you don't intend to shoot Blackwell—or whoever—out of his saddle."

She tucked her chin back with a sassy smile, still tracing the stitches on the pillow. "Well, I'd like to rope and hog-tie him, haul him home to his wife like a side of beef, and tell him the next time I found him cutting timber on my land, I was gonna tie him to a tree and leave him for the cougars."

Seth whistled through his teeth. "I hope I never get on your bad side. They teach you things like that at your fancy girls' school in Denver?"

She laughed. The trickling-creek laugh. "You know very well they did not. And you also know I've been roping since I was ten."

That he did.

All of a sudden, she jerked her head around, then jumped off the sofa and hurried to the stove. He hadn't noticed, but now he caught the aroma of fresh-baked peach pie. Good thing she'd made two, because he planned to eat one all by himself.

"Wash up." She looked over her shoulder with a smile. "Time to eat."

No, it wasn't. It was time to take a good hard look at his life and figure out how to get Abigale Millerton to share it with him.

~

Seth had been hungrier than he thought. After half a pie and two helpings of fried potatoes and pork that Abigale called Pop's hash, he leaned back from the table mostly a satisfied man. "That beat my cooking six ways from Sunday."

"That's tomorrow, you know."

"What is?"

"Sunday."

Shoot. His folks were probably wondering where he was. He'd ridden in to mail a couple of letters for his ma, then followed his gut to Millertons'. Hopefully she knew he was all right. She always claimed the Lord told her which way the wind was blowing.

Abigale set their plates in the sink and refilled his coffee.

He took his cup to the window at the front of the house, where he saw absolutely nothing except himself in the glass. The night was dark as the inside of one of Abigale's peach tins with the lid still on, but an inch of snow edged the windowsill and pane moldings.

He set his coffee on the hearth, tugged on his slicker, and grabbed the lantern. "I'm going for more wood."

Pop Millerton had built a stout home, for Seth hadn't felt the steady gusts that were drifting the snow onto what had drifted the night before and sweeping the ground bare.

He and Coop could make it home if they skirted the drifts, but it'd be a long, hard haul. And he didn't want to leave Abigale alone.

He made two trips, bringing in all the split wood and some smaller logs, then split a few from a bigger pile out behind the house. He'd tackle more tomorrow and stack it under the eaves. As much as he wanted to, he couldn't stay forever, but another night would ease his worry for her some.

Another night on the floor in front of the fire, dreaming about how to win her heart. Right now he figured it had a whole lot to do with helping her win what *she* wanted, which was freedom from poachers, if you could call 'em that. How did you prove someone's stealing your trees when the whole country grew the same kind?

'Cept those lodgepoles. They grew thick and stout on Millerton land, not in spindly doghair patches. Blackwell had a few acres that skirted around to the west, but not near the timber Abigale did.

Seth had cut his share of trees with his pa. Hard work it was, felling them, limbing them where they lay, then dragging them out on horseback with heavy chains, one at a time. If Blackwell was cutting timber, there'd be signs.

With winter rolling in, most of the mills had slowed to a stop, according to Hoot. But his Windsor was still running lodgepoles, he'd said.

Greed could twist a man into a fool, and there was a chance that a few clear days in a row might draw out Abigale's timber thief for one final run.

An itch started in the back of Seth's mind and settled into a warm spot right next to Abigale's scheme.

CHAPTER 8

Abigale finished washing the supper dishes and put them away. Breakfast would be more of the same since she had no eggs, so she was pleased that Seth had eaten heartily. She covered the remains of one pie with a napkin and set it on the table with the sugar and preserves, then put the other pie in the safe. Not that it would actually be safe if someone decided he was hungry in the middle of the night. Seth not only filled out Pop's clothing, he filled out Pop's capacity for food as well. Which was why she left a decoy on the table.

She settled onto the sofa, feet up, and tucked her skirt around them. The fire threw dancing shadows across the floor and onto Pop's chair where Seth stretched his legs to the hearth.

What if he hadn't shown up when he did? Would she even be alive?

Mams would have said the storm brought him here when Abigale needed him most and didn't know it. She'd say it was God's way to use a storm like that. The way He'd used Abigale's very first storm of losing her parents to bring her to the Millertons, who had no children of their own.

She picked up the cross-stitched pillow, heavy with memories. A small brown stain marred one corner, no doubt blood from where she'd hit her head. Tears stung the backs of her eyes, making it hard to read the words. She knew them by heart, but reading them and fingering the tiny stitches reminded her that Mams's faith had grown over time, just like the painstaking handiwork.

"'Trust in the LORD, and do good,'" she whispered into the stillness. A log burned through and fell, a comforting sound against the night. "'So shalt thou dwell in the land, and verily thou shalt be fed.'"

Dwell in the land—that was what Abigale wanted.

Somehow, having faith sounded easy when Mams had talked about it, yet Abigale knew for a fact that it wasn't.

Seth stirred and drew his feet in.

She'd forgotten he was there, so alone she was in her thoughts.

"You say something?"

"Just musing to myself."

He rubbed his hand over his face and up into his hair. "Didn't mean to doze off."

"It's all right. You were comfortable. You deserve to rest."

His eyes flashed a question, surprised that she would say such a thing. Perhaps it was their circumstances, alone together in a solid house that held out the weather. Or she was softening further toward him. Realizing there was more to Seth Holt than a bigger, stronger, annoyingly bossy friend.

He turned the chair toward her a little. "About your plan."

She shook her head. "It was silly. I see that now."

"I disagree."

Shocked, she stilled her fingers and locked on Seth's dark features, shadowed by the firelight behind him.

"With modifications."

So there it was. His typical assumption that he could improve upon her ideas. He'd been doing so for years.

Scooting the chair around until he faced her, he leaned forward, arms on his legs, mere inches from the edge of the sofa. "I suggest we go up there the next clear day we get and mark your trees."

He'd lost his mind, of course. And he'd said *we* twice. She wasn't sure how she felt about him using that word so much.

"And what would *we* mark them with? Ribbons and lace?"

Pain sparked in his eyes—quick as lightening—before he covered it with a smirk, but she rushed through the gap in his armor. "I'm sorry. I didn't mean to mock you, it's just, it's just …"

"A habit."

He'd nailed her, and she felt the blush of guilt rising in her cheeks.

Reaching for her hand, he let go a heavy sigh. Like a confession. "I fight the same habit, Abigale, but this time I'm serious."

Her pulse jumped at his strong fingers atop her own, the way his thumb idly rubbed the back of her hand.

She glanced down.

He let go.

Attempting to mend the breach, she asked, "What would we mark them with?"

"Paint."

"You're serious."

"As a grass fire."

He leaned back, hands gripping his knees, his long fingers squeezing in and out as if he molded the words as he spoke.

"My dad has reddish-brown paint left over from the barn. If I set it by the fire for a day or so, it'd warm up so we could smear it on the trees, high enough that it wouldn't be noticed by loggers in a hurry. Then I'd put a bug in Hoot's ear to keep a lookout for stolen trees. Honestly, it's a long shot, but it might work."

"I think it's brilliant."

"You do?"

"It's brilliant if I get to paint the trees. You can hold me on your shoulders." Her admission came at a high price to her pride, but she wasn't completely feather-headed. "When will you get the paint?"

"Same time I get a crate of hens and see if Ma will let me take one of her milk cows off her hands. I'm pretty sure she won't mind. That is, if you let me borrow your wagon and mare."

"Seth Holt, I could hug you." Impulsively she threw her arms around his neck and herself off balance.

He had to catch her to keep her from falling on the floor.

~

Deeper drifts sloped against the barn and outbuildings the next morning, but the wind had cleared enough ground that Seth was confident he could drive home and back before nightfall.

Abigale refused to go with him. She had it in her head that she wasn't leaving and probably feared he wouldn't bring her back.

And she was probably right, doggone it. Especially after he caught her in his arms last night.

Carrying her in the house when she was unconscious was one thing, but holding her while she was wide awake and laughing was something else altogether.

He shoved that memory aside and focused on making sure there was plenty of firewood in case he *didn't* make it back tonight. By the time he finished splitting a pile and stacking it inside on the hearth, he'd lost an hour of daylight but gained enough confidence to leave Abigale alone for the time being.

After checking Tess's harness, he went inside for his slicker.

Abigale approached him, a shallow basket in her hands, suspiciously pie-sized and covered with a checkered cloth. "Give this to your mother and tell her thank you for sharing her hens with me. I'll be sure and pay her back in the spring."

Judging by the wistful look on her face, she just might miss him while he was gone.

He accepted the basket and peeked under the cloth. "You don't need to do this, you know. Ma's happy to share."

"I know." Abigale rubbed her hands down the front of her apron, nervous-like. "But I want to."

"What if I eat it before I get to the ranch?" He couldn't resist teasing her, just enough to raise a little color in her cheeks.

"You'd better not, Seth Holt, if you expect to see any more where that came from." Her fists flew to her hips and perched there while she drilled him with her pretty eyes.

He set the basket aside and moved in closer. Took her gently by the shoulders. Drank in the way she smelled, all womanly and domestic. He didn't know whether to bargain or beg, so he dropped his voice and opted for bossy. "Don't you ride out to the tree line, huntin' trouble, while I'm gone."

Like hair on a wolf, her hackles rose. She stiffened, but didn't jut her chin. Just looked up at him from under her brows in a way that twisted his insides. "You come back to me."

He swallowed. Hard.

"I need those chickens."

Confounded woman. He grabbed the basket and stomped out to the wagon.

She came running after him. "Here, don't forget your slicker." She rolled it and shoved it under the seat. "I wouldn't want you to catch your death. Like I said, I need those—"

He looped an arm around her waist and pulled her close. She didn't resist but molded perfectly against him, her heart fluttering like a captive bird. Surprise rounded her eyes, not fear. Her lips parted, her breath caught, and he knew if he didn't leave right that minute, he might not ever leave.

CHAPTER 9

Abigale nearly fell.

Without so much as a goodbye or fare-thee-well, Seth climbed to the wagon seat and drove around the barn and out of sight.

Her breath returned on an afterthought, whispering up from deep inside. She drew a second one and told herself he was just lording it over her. Showing off. Having the last word, so to speak. She told herself there'd been no fire dancing in his eyes as they swept her mouth. No fire answering in her belly.

She'd never been a very good liar.

Hurrying to the corner of the barn, she watched him drive along the ranch road, cut across the range like he'd started to yesterday, and shrink until he was an ant in the distance, so far away she couldn't see him moving at all. He blended into the sweeping drifts and bare patches, leaving nothing but a longing in her heart.

She touched her lips, searching for proof that he'd been close enough to kiss her—but didn't. Proof that she hadn't dreamed the whole thing. But the only proof was her racing pulse that made the back of her head throb.

Chester yapped and pushed into her skirts with a whine.

She dropped down and rubbed behind his ears. "Did you see that, boy?" she whispered.

His pink tongue caught her chin.

"That man just drove away with half my good sense." She brushed off her apron as she straightened. "And he left less than that for you. He eats as much as Pop did, if not more."

Chester followed her in the house and plopped down by the hearth.

From the huge stack piled against the wall she added logs to the fire, then dropped into the big chair, reliving those minutes by the wagon and listening.

Seth did not return. He did not rein in at the house, barge through the door, and sweep her into his arms.

Such fantasy.

The fire snapped. Chester gave a long groan, indication of his old bones at rest.

Abigale was alone. Again.

So often she'd preferred it. Especially in Denver at the hall where she rarely found a moment to herself. But in Denver she had persevered with dreams of her high-country home. The peak. The high parks and the pines. This house.

Now here she was with it all around her, and it wasn't quite what she'd expected.

Chester sighed again, and sparks dashed up the chimney. The smell of coffee and fried pork lingered, and the prospects of a long, lonely day stretched before her.

Lonely and alone, she'd discovered, were two completely different concepts.

She hadn't felt bereft of friend and family when she'd first come back. Sad, yes. But energized for the work that faced her. Getting ready for winter after winter had already arrived was a daunting chore, but she'd welcomed the distraction. Now all she had was to sit and think and miss Pop even more.

And relive Seth's embrace.

She hugged her waist, recalled the strength of his arm around her, like a promise that nothing would ever come between them.

He wasn't the Seth Holt she'd grown up with, yet somehow he was.

What would she do when he returned? Fling herself into his arms or pretend that nothing had happened? No, she was as good at pretending as she was lying. Things would not be the same between them. An invisible barrier had been crossed, and she could no more go back than she could keep the sun from gilding the peak at dawn.

She went to the window, assuring herself the yard was empty, that he hadn't come back for something. A silly thought for certain. But she feared the flinging option might override the remains of her good sense if he did return so soon.

What would Mams say?

Immediately the answer came. "Mams would tell me to get busy."

Chester lifted his head at her commanding tone.

"I can't stand around getting all muddle-headed over some cowboy I've known all my life." A task definitely easier said than done.

"Come on, Chester. Want a dried biscuit with a little grease smeared on it?"

Chester evidently understood more than he let on and followed her to the kitchen, where she set a pan on the floor, broke biscuits into it, and poured grease over the top.

He'd be spoiled for sure, eating inside the house. Mams had never allowed it, but Abigale appreciated his company.

She untied and re-tied her apron, tucked loose hair behind her ear, and looked out the kitchen window.

Nope, Seth still wasn't coming this way. But he had to eventually. He'd left Coop here. That meant something, right? A man didn't leave his horse and saddle behind if he wasn't planning to come back for them.

Besides, Seth Holt kept his word. He'd bring those chickens.

A tingling sensation danced up her spine like sparks from the fire. *Chickens* was the last word on her lips. The last thing she'd said to him—or was about to say.

Looking around the kitchen, her gaze landed on the bread bowl. She'd make bread. That would busy her hands, which would busy her mind and help her think straight.

She took down the bowl and set the kettle on for warm water.

"What if his folks don't let him come back tonight?"

Chester finished the scraps and glanced her way.

"You're right. That's ridiculous. He's a grown man. All of twenty-two, with years of thinking for himself."

The dog plopped down beside the stove.

"But he might *have* to wait until tomorrow morning. It's not all that easy to get a cow to move at a lively pace." She waited for Chester's agreement.

He licked his jowls.

"Fine conversationalist you are."

She stopped talking to the dog and concentrated on what she was doing. Her favorite part of baking bread had always been the kneading, and she put all her pent-up energy into it until she had a smooth, satiny ball of dough turned into the bowl with a towel over the top.

"The day is young, Chester. The sky bright and clear, with very few clouds ringing the peak. Did you notice that earlier? There are no cloudbanks building yet. Not that they won't be by midday. So that means we should get going."

The dog sat up and cocked his head at her.

"I know what he said, but he can't just order me around."

She laid her apron over the back of a chair. "And I can't just sit around either. Not when it's such a beautiful day and there are horses outside and places to see. What do you say—you up for an outing?"

Chester made a throaty sound and turned his head away.

"Don't you scold me too."

Men! Impossible creatures.

At the bottom of the stairs, she paused. "I'll be down and ready to leave in two shakes of your feathery tale."

~

Seth thought he was losing his mind, for he'd sure enough gone and tossed his heart.

When he was far enough away from the barn, he glanced back. He couldn't see Abigale, which meant she couldn't see him. Good.

If she hadn't looked so dang pretty and perturbed, he might have gotten away without showing his hand.

But the memory of the moment made him want to go back and finish what he'd started. For all her fight and fire, Abigale Millerton was as sweet and soft as a new feather pillow.

The thought of her being alone prodded him on, and he flicked the reins. "Get on there, ol' girl. We're burnin' daylight and it's winter, so we've got none to spare."

Late-morning, he pulled up on his ma and Emmy stepping out of their wagon, just home from church. Pa nodded and drove to the barn. The dogs yapped and barked around the rig until Seth jumped down, and they wiggled up to him, whining their apologies.

Emmy ran into his arms. "Where have you been? I've been so worried about you. Course Ma wasn't, you know. She said you were somewhere safe. But it's been *forever*. Where were you?"

He gave his sister a quick kiss on the top of her head and reached for the pie.

"About time you showed you face."

"Yes, ma'am. Sorry about that, but I got waylaid by the storm." He looped an arm around his ma's shoulder.

Her gaze darted from the basket in his hands to the wagon and mare, and back to him. "You lose your horse?"

"No, ma'am. Coop's at the Millerton place where I sheltered." He kissed her on the cheek and handed her the basket. "This pie's from Abigale. To thank you for the chickens."

Emmy tugged on the basket and peeked in. "What chickens? And what kind of pie? Is it pumpkin? I *love* pumpkin."

His ma frowned as she lifted the napkin from Abigale's peach pie that he believed was as good as hers, though he wouldn't mention that part.

"Abigale Millerton is back at her grandfather's ranch? This time of year?"

"She is. I didn't know it when Coop and I headed for her barn. In fact, I didn't know it until their old dog hounded me out into the snow and wind, where I found Abigale in a heap by the barn."

"Sounds like we've got a story comin' for dinner. I take it this is Abigale's mare and buggy. Why didn't she come with you?"

"Yeah, why didn't she come?" Emmy tugged on his arm.

"Leave Seth be and take this inside, Emmy. Be careful you don't drop it. We'll have it with dinner."

At his ma's patient stalling, he tugged his hat off and scrubbed his head. "Because she's the most stubborn, infuriating gal this side of Pikes Peak."

His ma's face lit like it did when she was hiding a private joke.

"She won't leave the place. Got it in her head to stand off against some timber thief that's cutting her lodgepole."

His ma patted a hand over her heart. "I knew you were all right, but I sensed something was going on. Go ahead and turn the mare out with the horses, then clean up and you can tell us about it while we eat."

"I'll be leaving right away. I don't want Abigale on that spread all by herself. Not until we figure out who's cutting her trees."

His ma walked up the front porch steps and untied her bonnet. "Well, that's no surprise, son. You've dogged after that young woman for quite some time."

Ma meant well, but she sure had a way of taking him down a notch.

While he washed up in the kitchen, he filled his family in on Abigale's ladder-building plan. His pa chuckled into his coffee cup. "She may not carry Millerton blood in her veins, but she's sure enough got it in her head and heart."

As usual, his ma spread a fine table, and her beef stew, cornbread, and the peach pie hit the spot every time she served another helping.

"We have any mail?" she asked between peach slices.

"No, ma'am. But I posted your letters the day I left, though the storm may have held up the stage."

Pa picked up his coffee. "Tell me about this timber you think someone's cutting on Millerton land."

"That's the biggest problem—we just suspect it. Hoot Spicer does too. He wouldn't name names, but he said lodgepoles are still coming through the Windsor Mill when every other mill is shut down for winter."

Pa pushed his plate back with a nod at his wife.

She stood and rested a hand on his shoulder as she took his plate.

Seth's folks were always touching each other. Just seemed natural, to his way of thinking, and it made it hard for him to keep his hands to himself around Abigale. He'd sure enough failed in that regard today.

"I'd like to take that bucket of barn paint back with me so we can mark her trees. See if they come through the mill."

Emmy screwed up her face. "You're gonna paint trees *brown*? Aren't they already brown?"

Seth tweaked her nose and she giggled.

"I figure we might have a week or two left before winter settles in for good. If someone's greedy enough, they could ride into that timber for one last felling, especially if they think no one's living in the house."

"Don't you suppose they've seen the chimney smoke?"

Seth nodded. "Suppose so. I drove Abigale into Divide yesterday for supplies, so I'm sure word got out then too. That's when I talked to Hoot." He looked his pa square in the eye. "But I want to know as badly as she does. If I leave her over there by herself, she'll confront whoever's trespassing and get herself in a jackpot."

His pa took a swig of coffee.

"She should come here," Emmy said.

"Scrape soap in the dishpan for me, Emmy." Ma refilled his father's coffee cup and tried to fill Seth's.

He covered it with his hand. "No, thanks."

"So you want chickens," she said. "Moving them in this weather might upset them, you know. Keep them from laying. But I've got a half dozen you can take. Once they settle, you should get eggs. If not, you'll get chicken stew."

Her eyes sparkled as she rejoined her husband at the table and took his hand.

Seth wanted that kind of companionship, and he wanted it with Abigale. His ma was right about that too. He'd been loving Abigale for a long time. He just hadn't admitted it to himself because he was afraid she'd marry some banker or lawyer in Denver rather than come back home.

"Can you spare one of your milk cows? Ernestine's gone dry, but we can breed her come spring."

"Oh, yes, please," Emmy cut in. "That'd be one less to milk every morning."

"Who do you think is helping himself to Millertons' lodgepole pine?" Pa shot Seth a look.

"Blackwell. His place borders to the southwest. But he doesn't have as much timber, or as good a stand as Millerton."

78

His ma's expression sobered. "You be careful, son. He's not a gracious man."

~

Not only did Seth's folks give him a small crate of hens and return Abigale's basket and pie pan full of eggs, his ma tied a young milker to the back of the wagon and his pa laid in a hunk of salted beef.

"Appreciate it, Pa. I know I'm leaving you short-handed, but I have to make sure Abigale is safe and has everything she needs before I come back."

His father gripped him on the shoulder and gave it a squeeze. "You're a good man, Seth. But be wise. Don't go lookin' for a fight that isn't yours. Bring her here if you can, let things smooth over till spring."

"And bring her before Christmas." His ma came off the porch and looped her arm through her husband's. "She shouldn't spend the holiday all by herself with no family. Tell her we'd love to have her."

If only it were that easy.

CHAPTER 10

The higher Abigale rode, the deeper the snow, and she regretted bringing Chester along. The old dog struggled to climb out every time he broke through the crusted top, but she knew he wouldn't go back on his own.

As they continued, Seth's warning stirred through her. *Don't you ride out to the tree line, huntin' trouble, while I'm gone.*

Her shoulders tightened. She wasn't hunting trouble, she was simply riding across her property, riding in the general direction of the lodgepole pines that flanked the mountain. And it was only prudent that Pop's fully loaded Henry rested in the scabbard. One did not ride into the mountains unprepared.

In spite of the crystal-blue sky, she was grateful she'd piled her braid under a woolen scarf and wrapped one of Pop's silk neckerchiefs around her throat. His hat stayed on with the added bulk, and the silk kept her warm. Pop's heavy coat did too, as well as Seth's words that rose inside her like hot steam from the kettle.

Though she accused him of being bossy, he'd never said anything so pointed unless danger was attached.

She fingered the scar at her left eyebrow, earned by her stubborn refusal to listen once before. He'd warned her

80

about descending the north side of Aspen Falls, the slick-rock footholds too far apart for her twelve-year-old legs. The same year he'd gotten the gray scarf, and unhesitatingly wrapped it around her head to stem the bleeding. Never had he complained about the brown stain left behind.

On a whim, she turned off the path and headed for the waterfall, hoping it was as beautiful as she remembered in winter. Frozen solid in an everlasting descent.

Only the horse crunching through snow broke the stillness, for Chester followed behind now, finding it easier on his old bones, she supposed. An occasional jay or squirrel scolded as they passed, and the pristine beauty of the land soothed Abigale's sense of loss.

People came and went, but the land—the land was forever.

All the world was white, it seemed, other than sky. Aspen trees huddled stark and bare, and cloaked evergreens dusted her with sparkling powder, branches lifting when their heavy loads slid away.

Without its summer voice giving notice, she came upon the falls by surprise. Beyond a stand of young pines, it hung like liquid glass against the rocky ledge, clear in places, pale blue or gray in others. Frozen yet still moving, a faint trickle whispered from beneath the icy mantel.

She stopped and dismounted. The horse blew impatiently, raising a breathy cloud. Chester came up beside her, and she bent to hug his neck.

"Isn't is beautiful?" she whispered, unwilling to disturb the peace of the place.

The horse lifted its head, ears sharp, trained toward the south. Chester did the same, looking into the thickets and forest that surrounded them. And that's when she heard it—

the snap of limbs, cracking like gunshots in the clear air, increasing in intensity until they ended in a final heavy crash.

Silence followed. No bird, no scurrying critter.

The horse blew again, and she gently covered its muzzle with her gloved hand.

Someone had felled a tree.

Swinging into the saddle, she turned from the falls, but not back the way they had come. Instead, she headed straight for the sound, through the forest at a slower but steady pace. Whoever had cut the tree would be busy stripping its branches and making enough noise to cover her approach.

Nor would they expect anyone to come in from above. With a touch of the reins, she aimed her mount farther up the slope and into the thicker tree stands.

As they climbed, she crossed clearings through which the wide park below spread out like a snowy blanket. A dark pocket of buildings marked Divide, muddy roads spoking from its hub. A handful of barns scattered across the valley, the nearest one her own, its roof a solid white slab that securely covered her winter feed, thanks to Seth.

Voices carried on the clear air, punctuated by the snap of an axe, the dull scrape of a saw limbing the pine. It wouldn't be easy dragging it out. One of their horses had to be stout, likely a draft animal that could pull the chained dead weight.

Near a rocky outcropping, she stopped and listened.

"Wrap it up, boys."

Abigale's heart lurched to her throat.

Harsh and heavy, the voice was unlike that of any teacher or student she'd known. Often as a child, she shrank from it on Sunday mornings when the owner bent low and peered at Abigale with cold, dark eyes to ask, "How's the little orphan today?"

Her grandmother's whole body would stiffen and she'd squeeze Abigale's hand. "Our granddaughter is right as rain on a summer's eve and twice as pretty." Then she'd stomp into the church house, dragging Abigale with her.

Once, Abigale looked over her shoulder and saw the bold, sneering face, an elbow nudging a snicker from a scrawny son.

A sudden gust danced through the trees, singing in the towering lodgepoles and brushing a chill across Abigale's face. She looked up to see full-bellied clouds scudding overhead. They'd soon bunch against the mountain, joining forces in a snowy onslaught.

She slid the Henry from the scabbard, dismounted, and loosely tied the horse to a thicket. Her hand, palm down, and a whispered "stay" dropped Chester to his belly.

Several yards away, she tucked into an old snag, sighted the crown of a tree near two men sawing limbs, and squeezed the trigger.

Sharp and clear, the target snapped. One man cursed.

Her lever action didn't give them time to think before her second shot hit a lower branch.

"Let's go!" the voice yelled.

Abigale chambered another round.

Three men scrambled at the order, one onto the back of a draft horse dragging a chain, and two into a wagon. Saws and axes were left behind.

The man on the drag horse took off with the wagon following fast. The other rider reined around and stared up into the brush, hard face unmistakable, even at this distance, as were the proud set of broad shoulders and large hands that roughly handled the horse.

Abigale waited a good long while before moving from the snag, listening as the startled thieves bounced their wagon over the mountain's shoulder. Commending Chester, she slid the Henry home and mounted, then circled around the fallen tree and came in from the north. She couldn't safely carry the saw, but two axes were easily tethered to the back of her saddle before she followed the clear trail that cut through snow, churning mud and rocks. By then, the sun was a thin memory behind gray quilting, and fine flakes had begun to fall.

Abigale raised the collar on Pop's coat and pulled his neckerchief over her nose and mouth. Nearing her property line, she turned for home. Chester followed in her wake.

If only there were some way to prove what she'd seen today. Otherwise, it was her word against theirs.

Blackwell wasn't among the thieves, only his hired hands. Abigale had seen that clearly. But he didn't need to be there. Not when the one running the show was his wife.

~

Seth made better time back to the Millertons' than he'd expected. Though he might have driven Tess harder than she was used to.

He unhitched the mare, then cooled her out and rubbed her down. Water and feed lured her to her stall, and while he was at it, he fed Coop and the other horses, Ernestine, and the new milker. He'd have to come back and milk after he carried the—

Other horses. He ran out to the corral and checked the pasture. No animals were down.

One was *gone*.

His gut twisted like a kinked rope.

No smoke curled from the chimney when he passed the house on his way to the root cellar with the beef. But a serious case of mad curled inside his chest, and he busted three eggs in his hurry to get them in the house.

Sure enough, the hearth was cold. It'd been cold a long time.

And the Henry was missing from its place above the mantel.

Blasted, bull-headed woman had gone and done exactly what he'd told her not to.

He built a fire, then pushed the chair and sofa farther back into the room in case a sap pocket snapped out an ember in his absence.

The cloud cover that laid against the mountain when he'd driven in had dropped considerably. Fat flakes were falling, and Coop wasn't all that happy to be saddled and riding out in it, but Seth wasn't going to sit by the fire and wait for Abigale to get home.

He struck out toward the mountain, but turned back for Pop's shotgun.

With fresh snow falling, Seth had no trail to follow. Only his instincts, and they were a poor match for the expanse of forest and mountain shoulder that loomed before him. In less than thirty minutes, it'd be dark as the inside of Abigale's root cellar.

Which way'd she go, Lord?

The lodgepole stretched a long swath that he couldn't cover in the dark, but that wasn't the image that came to him. Rather, he saw the falls. Aspen Falls, he and Abigale had called it when they were kids. It was tucked back in a rocky cleft where the white-barked trees spilled out like a gold river in the fall.

He supposed it was a matter of trust. He'd asked for help, now he had to trust he'd heard right, so with a touch of his heel, he turned Coop toward the northern edge of the timber.

Why did Abigale do this to him? Did she hate him? Did she want to drive him crazy with longing or just drive him off?

His pa had told him to be wise. Seth knew what that meant. Slow down and pay attention. Don't go off half-cocked. He shifted the shotgun lying across his lap, grateful he'd had enough sense to see it was loaded and put extra shells in his coat pocket.

Bears hibernated. Cats didn't. Catamount Creek was so named for a reason, and this was the time of day the big cats hunted, when their eyes saw better through the falling dark than anyone else's. A scattergun wouldn't drop one. He'd need daylight for a shot like that, not to mention a rifle. But he had a chance at scaring one off if need be.

"God, help us."

Coop's ear flicked back at Seth's voice, a foreign sound in the snowy silence.

Seth paid close attention to the horse, for Coop would sense danger before he did, and it could mean the difference between life and death.

On the heels of that thought, Coop lifted his head and snorted, ears pointing straight ahead. He wasn't nervous, didn't twitch and side-step, but he definitely knew someone—or something—was coming.

Seth slid the gun off his lap with his right hand, held it against his thigh, muzzle angled down, and slowed Coop's walk. Movement caught his eye, and he squinted through the snowfall. Someone was riding this way. A man, hat low, shoulders hunched against the cold. A small man. Seth reined aside into the trees and waited.

If he hadn't recognized Pop's old hat and coat, he wouldn't have known it was Abigale riding the bay. He wasn't all that familiar with their horses, but he'd know that hat anywhere. He was half ready to give a whoop and a holler to know she was safe, and half mad as a hornet that she'd ridden off by herself. If he was a kid, he'd kick Coop's side and chase her home, give her a fright for doing what she'd done to him.

But he wasn't a kid. He was a man in love with an infuriatingly independent woman. And winning her wasn't going to be easy.

He nudged Coop onto the trail.

Abigale drew up, suddenly straight as a barn board, eyes round as dollars and colorless in the near dark. A neckerchief covered her mouth and nose.

"Goin' somewhere?" He couldn't keep the growl from his voice. Anger did that to him, and at the moment anger was winning over relief.

The bay danced backward at Abigale's tight draw on the reins, and her free hand went to her chest. "Seth Holt, you scared me half to death."

"Good. We're even."

With that, he turned for the house.

She followed, subdued for once. He heard only the hooves of her horse behind him as they cut through the silent woods. Until he didn't.

Whirling Coop around, he found her missing. *Missing*! Did he have to tie a lead on her horse?

"Seth!"

At the fear in her voice, he dug his heels in and raced up the trail. She wasn't far.

"He's gone. Chester's gone. We have to go back."

The snow fell heavier now, laying down a thick blanket. "You brought Chester with you?"

"I know. It was foolish of me."

Seth snorted. That wasn't the only foolish thing she'd done, but pointing that out wasn't going to help matters. "When did you notice him missing?"

"Just now—a few seconds ago. I hadn't paid attention until you met us on the trail. I just assumed he was following in my steps like he had been."

"Stay here. I'll ride back a ways, see if I can find him."

No surprise when she gathered herself and turned her horse. "I'm going with you."

Arguing with her was pointless and time consuming, and at the moment time was what they didn't have.

Fresh snow nearly filled their trail that grew fainter the farther they rode. The old dog must have fallen, unable to make it in the cold. Seth felt the loss deep inside, but the dog wasn't worth Abigale's safety. He reined in.

"Abigale."

She rode past him.

He heeled Coop into a lunge and sprang around in front of her. "Abigale—I understand Chester is important to you. But he's not worth your life."

At a whimper, they both turned their heads.

Seth swung the gun barrel forward and gave Coop his head, but the horse began to blow and quake, shied to the right.

A snowy mound on the trail uttered a weak growl. Seth raised the gun and aimed across his horse, into the brush on the left.

A blur sprang to the trail.

Seth fired.

Coop reared at the unexpected explosion.

Seth fired the second round and reloaded as Coop danced beneath him, unsettled by the gunshot as well as the lion. But as far as Seth could tell, the cat was gone. For the time being.

Abigale jumped down and ran to Chester, lifted him from the ground, but couldn't remount with his weight. Seth held the dog while she stepped up, then laid him across her lap and swung back into the saddle.

Without saying a word, they turned for the house with Abigale in the lead and Seth watching Coop's ears, as well as over his own shoulder.

Chapter 11

Abigale couldn't see through her tears, but she felt Chester shivering where he lay by the fire as she toweled him dry. Seth had settled him on a quilt while Abigale unsaddled her horse. If he'd seen the axes, she'd never hear the end of it.

Taking care with the sores on Chester's head, she gingerly dabbed where buckshot left little bare patches. The mountain lion had grazed him but hadn't had a chance to dig in its claws or fangs, thanks to Seth's clear thinking.

If Chester died, she'd never forgive herself. He was all she had left of her family.

Coffee filled the house with a comforting aroma that did little to ease Abigale's guilt. Seth clattered around in the kitchen and cracked eggs into a skillet of hot grease that sizzled and popped.

He'd kept his word and brought the eggs.

New tears joined those already streaming down her cheeks. Seth Holt had not only kept his word, he'd gone the extra mile—or three or four—again expending hard work, loyalty, and kindness on her behalf.

She leaned over Chester, consoled by his wet-dog smell as she ran the towel over his legs and side.

"Here, drink this." Not so much an order as an offering, Seth handed her a mug and dropped beside her on the floor. Legs crossed like always, he held a plate of scrambled eggs in his other hand.

"I should never have taken him with me."

Seth made no reply.

With her sleeve she wiped her eyes, then glanced to read his thoughts, expecting agreement. Reprimand. She saw neither.

He handed her the plate. "Eat."

"I can't."

"Need me to feed you?" Not an offering this time.

"This is no time to be boss—"

"This is no time to pass out on me." Humor did not mark his expression. "You eat half, I'll eat half."

She took the plate.

"If he doesn't make it, Abigale, it won't be for lack of your care. Age takes us all if something else doesn't do it first, and there's nothing you can do to stop that."

Part of her wanted to believe that wisdom, but part of her doubted. She could have postponed her grandfather's passing if she'd been here to help. And she could have locked Chester in the barn before she left this morning.

Seth boldly reached for her coffee cup and drank from it. "Everything that happens isn't your fault."

His words squeezed fresh tears, and she scarcely made out the eggs he'd scrambled. He was scrambling her heart as well, showing a side of himself she'd not imagined but for which she was grateful.

After two bites, she handed him the plate. "Thank you."

He grumped. "Don't like my cooking, I see."

With a hand on his knee, she stalled his sarcasm. "Thank you for what you said, as well as for what you've done. The eggs yes, but mostly for coming after me. I couldn't bear losing Chester like that—on account of my stubbornness."

Seth laid the plate aside and drew her into his arms, holding her awkwardly against his side, but holding her. She wanted to be nowhere else than right there, close to him, feeling the beat of his heart, the security of his arms. He had become much more to her than a neighboring rancher's son.

When he kissed the top of her head, his tenderness nearly undid her.

"Come home with me. Spend Christmas with us. Emmy and Ma want you to. Even Pa said so."

She straightened and looked into his warm gaze, a dark forest in the fire's light. Did *he* want her there? Temptation called. "But who will look after the animals?"

"We'll take them with us. Drive 'em home for the winter."

He picked up the plate and shoveled in a mouthful of eggs. "The timber-cutting will stop soon in this weather."

"I saw them."

His fork halted. "Who was it?"

"Not Blackwell."

With a huff he shook his head. "I was so sure." He took another bite.

"It was his wife."

Seth miscalculated his swallow. Abigale slapped him on the back and handed him her coffee. Catching his breath, he set down the plate and cup and focused on her completely. "You're sure."

"Absolutely. I'd know that voice anywhere. And I saw her. Dressed like a man, but I recognized her."

"Was Blackwell himself there?"

Abigale shook her head. "No. Just his wife and three hired hands. One might have been their son, I'm not sure. He's not as memorable as his mother."

Seth stared into the fire, his face a map of thoughts connecting, jumping, tumbling upon each other until finally he voiced what Abigale had already concluded. "She won't make another run. Not now. I'm surprised she tried it again, though I'd hoped we could mark the trees before another cutting."

Abigale hoped he wouldn't ask what she'd done when she found them.

"Where were they?"

"Just south of the falls."

He took her hand and folded his around it, then kissed her fingers.

The gesture sent a thrill of energy through her. "It's beautiful, the waterfall. Frozen yet living beneath the surface. I rode up there to see it and was there when I heard the tree fall."

"So you didn't ride out to check on the timber?"

Unable to hold his scrutiny, she dropped her gaze. "I did at first. I couldn't just sit here and do nothing. It is my land, you know. I'm responsible."

He grumbled and it resonated from his chest and into her hand through his, but he didn't let go of her.

"Once I got up there, where we used to ride, I wasn't thinking about the timber. Not until they felled the tree." Angered all over again, she tried to pull away, but he wouldn't let her, so she resigned herself to his hold.

"They didn't even take it from the edge. Cut it right out of the middle, crushing saplings and snapping branches of nearby trees as it fell. That's what first caught our attention—the horse and Chester and me. The snapping. Like gunfire through the woods."

Poor choice of words on her part. She prayed he wouldn't pick up on that.

He frowned, as if studying their linked fingers, turning their hands over until hers was on top. "Is that where you picked up the two axes tied on the back of your saddle?"

She flinched.

Still, he didn't let go. His green gaze latched onto her even tighter, shadowed like the corners of the room. Smoldering like a banked fire.

Please, please don't ask about Pop's rifle.

"Did they see you?"

She exhaled. "No."

"Can you be sure?"

"Yes. Well—no. But we were still as death, several yards back in the trees near a granite outcropping above them, and they were making such a racket they couldn't have heard our approach." Though they clearly heard her rifle.

He looked away, nodding slowly, thinking silent thoughts she wished he'd share.

A log shifted on the fire, and his gaze slid to her again. Through her, really. Back through all their growing-up years, their scrapes and spills. Their arguments and adventures. "Will you come home with me?"

How could she not?

Before sunup, Seth had the fire roaring and Chester lapping water from a shallow dish. Frankly, he was surprised Abigale hadn't stayed on the hearth with the old fella, but Seth had promised he'd watch him and convinced her to sleep upstairs in a real bed. He'd taken the sofa.

His neck reminded him how short that sofa was as he shrugged into his coat and clapped his hat on. He'd feed early and milk the cow so they could start at sunup. It'd be hard going after last night's storm. Much harder than getting Abigale's agreement had been.

She'd surprised him, but he hadn't pressed his luck by asking questions. He doubted that meeting up with the mountain lion had influenced her. She didn't frighten easily from critters. And she loved that old dog of her grandparents, but that wasn't it either. There was a different light in her eyes when she'd nodded her consent. And Seth believed it had everything to do with the fact that he'd *asked* her.

He didn't press her, or bribe her, or threaten to throw her in the wagon. He didn't tell her what she ought to do. He simply asked, and she agreed.

A lesson he needed to remember.

When he came in from the barn, she had coffee on and breakfast frying. Her yellow braid hung down her back with a blue ribbon tied on the end, and an old skirt she used to wear fit her a whole lot better than it did before she went away two years ago.

He left his hat and coat on hooks by the door and washed at the sink, grateful for the icy water in light of his warming insides.

"You're out early."

"Yes, ma'am. Sooner we're ready, the sooner we can leave."

"Did you milk the cow? And please don't say *ma'am* again."

He grinned. "I did. On the ground. Wasteful, but necessary for today."

"Sit down, then, and we'll eat before we pack up the kitchen."

He stalled behind his chair, and she cut him a look. "I am not leaving everything I bought to the mice and whatever else will work its way in here while I'm gone. And I'm sure your mother will appreciate my contributions since I'll be another mouth to feed."

What Abigale ate wouldn't keep one of her imagined mice alive, but he didn't argue.

She set their plates and the coffee pot on the table, then joined him and held out her hand.

He didn't need to be told twice. He wrapped his fingers around hers and bowed his head. "Thank you, Lord, for seeing us safely home last night and for this food. Amen."

She squeezed his hand before slipping hers free, and it stirred the earlier warmth more than her hot coffee, eggs, and fried potatoes. So much for dousing the fire.

The sun peeked over the summit as they loaded the last of her stores. While Seth greased the axles, hitched up Tess, and saddled Coop, Abigale brought quilts and satchels out of the house and baskets full of he didn't know what. But he didn't care if she wanted to bring the table and chairs. She was going with him. Willingly.

They secured the door and shuttered all the windows, including those in the barn. Seth laid Chester on a bed

Abigale made behind the wagon seat, then stuffed confused hens in the chicken coop.

He left the paint behind.

Abigale bundled up in her grandfather's coat, hat, and a thick scarf, then climbed up and drove out along the ranch road, looking nothing at all like the proper young woman Seth had taken into town a few days ago.

He opened the corral gate and the animals followed the wagon with him trailing behind. Driving the little herd would be a lot easier than driving the wagon, but Abigale was up to it. Made him puff up like a rooster just thinking about it.

He trotted up beside her, his protective instincts stronger than his pride. "You want me to drive the wagon and you can push the livestock?"

Her glare was answer enough, and he reined around, choking on a chuckle.

They cut across the valley, edging the higher drifts, and the sun was straight overhead before they pulled in the yard at the Lazy H.

Nothing lazy about it other than the lying-down letter that made up his family's brand.

His pa had seen them coming, for he stood at the corral gate, holding it open. Ma waited on the porch with Emmy, a shawl wrapped tight around her shoulders and a big smile on her face. He couldn't hear what she said when Abigale jumped from the wagon, but the way she and his sister wrapped their arms around her told him plenty.

"I'm glad you made it, son. There's a big one blowing in tonight. I feel it in my bones."

"You're usually right, Pa," Seth conceded, taking in the cloud cover bunching up against the east side of the valley.

His pa forked hay into a couple of troughs and pushed the cows inside the barn. Seth unsaddled Coop and rubbed him down, then turned him out with the other horses before helping the women unload the wagon.

His ma clucked and fussed. "Why in the world did you bring all this food, Abigale? You have enough here to feed a branding crew for a month."

Abigale blushed, but Seth didn't think anyone realized it but him. He knew her every expression and all the shades she could turn.

"I don't know how long I'll be here, Mrs. Holt, and I intend to pay my way."

"It's Ida, dear. Ida and Ben. We're just family, that's all."

Seth's heart swelled until it nearly cracked his ribs. He hefted out the hens and stomped off toward the chicken house before he made a blubbering fool of himself.

"Emmy," his ma called. "You go with Seth and show him where to set those hens."

Like they needed directions inside their old roost. Ma was getting rid of a little pitcher with big ears.

"I didn't recognize her!" Emmy's surprise drew her up next to him, breathless with excitement. "Is she really going to stay for Christmas? I heard Ma and Pa talking to you about it at dinner, you know. How wonderful it will be to have another girl here for Christmas! I can't wait to ask her—"

"Emma June."

She scowled up at him.

"Abigale is not a girl, she's a woman." *Boy howdy.* "And don't go bending her ear with everything that rattles through your head. Mind your manners."

"Well, you should mind yours too. You know I don't like *Emma June.*"

Which was exactly why he'd used it, to get her attention. "Open the gate for me."

She complied and he lifted the coop lid. The hens hopped out and fluttered around their former companions, raising a ruckus to rival Emmy and her babbling.

"You're sweet on her, aren't you?"

He clapped the coop shut and carried it out, then latched the chicken-yard gate. "That hen? What's got into you, girl?"

"You're not funny, you know."

He yanked one of her braids.

She took a swing at his arm. "Cut it out or I'm telling Ma you're sweet on Abigale."

"It's *Miss* Abigale to you."

"I *knew* it!"

She ran back to the house, pigtails and skirt a-flying. "Ma-ah!"

Emmy wouldn't be spouting anything Ma didn't already know.

CHAPTER 12

The Holt ranch house wasn't all that different from Abigale's grandparents' home, aside from the extra rooms on the second floor. She fully expected to share a bed with Emmy, but Mrs. Holt led her to the end of the hall, where a squeaky door opened into a stuffy room.

At the window, Mrs. Holt moved the curtains aside and raised the sash. "Just for a few minutes, to let the old air out and the new in."

She turned with a warm smile. "Haven't had a guest in such a long time, that I forget to air this room out. I hope you don't mind. The bed clothes are clean, though I should probably take the pillows and quilts outside for a good beating."

"I'm sure they're fine, Mrs.—I mean Ida. Thank you all the same."

Seth's mother swept both hands across a star quilt folded at the foot of the bed. "Let me know if you need help settling in. I'll send Emmy up with fresh water after a while, but I warn you, she will talk your ears off. Scoot her out when you've had enough."

Abigale chuckled, remembering nervous newcomers at Wolfe Hall with the same propensity. "Thank you, but she's no bother at all. You've been most generous."

The simple bed with low headboard and turned posts was similar to what Abigale had slept in at the school, though big enough for two people.

At the sudden wash of heat in her cheeks, she set her satchel on a sewing rocker, her back to Ida Holt without appearing rude, then took off Pop's hat and the heavy scarf.

"It can be warm up here, which is certainly a benefit in the winter." Ida dropped the window sash but pushed the curtains farther open. "I've always favored this view of the ranch."

Abigale moved to Ida's shoulder, agreeing with her observation. The barn and outbuildings stood in good repair at right angles to the house, creating a large yard. A fringe of pine and spruce hemmed the northern edge, and no doubt helped block the wind.

Ida rested a hand on her arm, voice quiet and welcoming. "I'm truly glad you came, Abigale. No one should be alone at Christmas."

Abigale blinked several times and forced a smile, unwilling to shed tears at the woman's gracious hospitality. It was the familiarity that stung the sharpest, for there was nothing strange about Ida Holt. Abigale had spent many a day here as a young girl, wondering if her mother might have looked and acted like Seth's—hair in a neat bun, face quick to smile and laugh or frown and scold. But she'd had no picture of her parents, only a child's memory thinned over the years by the two loving faces of Mams and Pop.

"Thank you," she managed.

With a light pat of her hand, Ida went to the washstand for the pitcher. "I'll send Emmy with clean towels as well. But remember what I told you. She's a chatterbox."

When the door closed behind her hostess, Abigale slumped to the bed, exhausted. She'd been so busy since arriving home, she'd not given serious thought to Christmas, other than to acknowledge that she missed her grandfather fiercely. Secretly, she was glad Seth had persisted. She'd have people around her during the holiday, a temporary family at best. But even though it wasn't hers, it was as close as any could be.

She fell back across the bed, both grief and gratitude heavy on her heart. Her eyes closed with confidence that Seth would see to Chester. A few quick winks were all she needed. Just a moment of rest, and she'd be good as new.

Within minutes, a squeaking hinge raised her.

"Did I wake you?" Dark brown braids dangled below a youthful face hoping indeed that Abigale was completely awake.

"I'm glad you did, Emmy. I can't be sleeping the day away with so much to do."

The girl read Abigale's comment as invitation and entered with the full pitcher. A few drops of water spotted her skirt and the floral carpet as she crossed the room.

"Mama said you might be sleeping." She set the pitcher in its matching bowl and transferred two towels from her arm to the rod on the washstand, then joined Abigale on the bed with a sigh.

"This is such a fancy room. Much prettier than mine. Mama said when I'm older I can maybe move into this one." She gave a little bounce on the mattress, then looked up quickly.

"That is, if you're not still here."

Abigale held in a full laugh and drew Emmy's braids over her shoulders. "You have nothing to worry about.

I shall be long gone by then." She paused and drummed the fingers of one hand against her chin. "How old are you now? Fifteen?"

"Pfftt—I wish! I'm only ten. And it will be forever before I've grown enough for this room."

"No, it won't, little one. Time flies much faster than you realize when you're young, so enjoy every minute of it. Why, when I was your age, your brother and I were traipsing all over this country, riding and exploring, and getting into arguments. It seems like only yesterday."

She clamped her lips tight, fearing she had shared too much information with the innocent child.

Emmy gave another little bounce. "I know all about that. Seth told me how you could ride and rope and even shoot almost as good as him."

"Almost?" How easily Abigale was drawn into a competitive mood, so typical of Seth Holt and his teasing.

"Wanna know a secret?" Emmy looked up from the corner of her eye, legs swinging up and bouncing back against the mattress and bed frame.

"Is it a very important secret, one you should not share?" Abigale had no desire to hear Holt family matters that were none of her business. She had enough concerns of her own.

Emmy waved Abigale's question away. "No. It's just about Seth."

Oh. Well then. Curiosity lifted its head, ravenous and reckless. "In that case,"—she crossed her heart and leaned in closer—"I promise not to tell."

Emmy giggled and cupped her hand around her mouth as if someone else might overhear. "He's sweet on you."

Abigale gulped at the revelation and was powerless to stop the flush rising in her neck and into her jawline. She fussed with her hair, hoping her hands would hide the worst of it. "How do you know? Did he tell you?"

The idea that Seth Holt confided in a sister less than half his age was not one Abigale relished.

"He doesn't have to tell me." Emmy jumped off the bed and assumed a very dignified air. "I just know these things."

Abigale covered her mouth, refusing to let laughter wound the little girl. After a moment's struggle for composure, she stood. "I see."

"That's it exactly," Emmy said on her way out the door. "All you have to do is look at him. You can see it all over his face."

Perhaps Abigale hadn't been looking at Seth with the right eyes.

She went to the window and discovered she'd rested longer than a few minutes. Dusk had settled over the ranch, hemmed in with a gentle snowfall. Seth and his father led animals into the barn, then shuttered windows and closed the big double doors.

Her stomach fluttered and her heartbeat kicked up just watching Seth. He moved about with purpose, a controlled grace in his long strides, and something about it appealed to her. *He* appealed to her.

Again she touched her lips, remembering how close he'd been—as if he meant to kiss her. Had he? He'd made no similar move since he'd returned with the chickens, but how could he when he'd been busy chasing off mountain lions, rescuing Chester, and moving all her stock and stores to his family's ranch?

Emmy may not have seen that embrace—thank heavens—but she insisted she knew her brother's feelings.

Abigale feared for her own emotions, for she wore them on her sleeve like a roadmap, according to Mams and Pop.

How was she going to spend Christmas in the Holt family home without letting them all know about her growing affection for Seth?

~

Pa was right again.

After supper, Seth tromped through nearly a foot of snow, double-checking the livestock. He and Pa had gotten everything settled just in time. Seemed to be a common theme lately.

He'd shown up at Millertons' not long after Abigale had fallen. Thwarted a lion's attack on Chester. And gotten Abigale and her animals here before this storm hit. From the looks of it, they might be socked in for days.

Maybe it was all a sign that he had just enough time to ask Abigale to marry him. If what he'd learned in the last two days held true, it was that simple. *Ask* her.

And he'd scare himself up a bear or two while he was at it, wrestle 'em down, and make her a rug from the hides. He screwed his hat down tighter, raised the collar of his coat, and went hunting the axe.

After stacking a wall of wood on the back porch, he stretched a rope to the barn, another one to the outhouse, and a third to the woodpile. At the back door, he stomped snow from his boots before entering, pulled them off inside, and hooked his hat and coat by the door.

His family sat by the hearth, Abigale with them, Chester at her feet. The old dog was lying on his belly and looking around as if unsure of where he was. Abigale leaned over and stroked his back, whispering against his ear. The dog's tail thumped in response.

"Did you see that?" She looked up as Seth drew another chair next to her. "Did you see his tail?"

"I did." He rubbed behind the dog's ears, careful of telltale buckshot sores. It could have been so much worse.

Abigale's eyes fluttered like she had a spec in one, and her voice dropped to a whisper. "Thank you for saving him, Seth." The shine of her gaze said a mountain more, but he'd not go there with his folks in hearing distance.

"How'd you save him, Seth?"

Leave it to Emmy to drag every last detail out into the open.

Ma dug through her mending basket. "Yes, we'd enjoy hearing that story as well, if you don't mind, Abigale. Forgive us if we're being nosy." She offered her friendliest smile for Abigale's benefit, but Seth recognized the tone that said, "Cough it up, and cough it up right now."

Abigale's face went a shade lighter, and he figured she was hesitant about mentioning what she saw in the woods.

"It's all right." He lowered his voice. "They already know about your trees. Pa's paint, remember?"

"Oh, yes. All right." She pushed at her hair, a clear sign she was nervous.

"I rode up to the waterfall yesterday, and Chester went with me. While we were there, we heard a tree fall and tracked the sound to where someone was limbing it, getting ready to drag it out."

Pa's gaze flicked to Seth and back. "Did you see who it was?"

Seth signaled Abigale to go ahead.

"It was Mrs. Blackwell."

His ma looked thunderstruck. "Charlotte?"

"Yes, ma'am. She had three men with her. Hired hands, I suppose. One might have been her son, but I couldn't be sure."

Pa rubbed the side of his jaw. "How do you know it was her?"

Abigale bucked a little, rising to the challenge. Seth couldn't help but admire her pluck when it wasn't directed at him.

"I'd know that voice anywhere."

Ma let out a disgusted huff. "You and me both, Abigale."

"But what about Chester? What happened to him?" Emmy stuck on an idea like a tick on a hound.

"He followed me." Abigale leaned over and stroked his side as if he were the most precious thing in her life. "But it was late by the time we headed back. He's old and tired, and when it started snowing, it must have been too much for him to keep up with me. I didn't know he'd fallen behind until Seth met us on the trail."

Her voice broke on the last word, and every head in the room turned in Seth's direction except hers.

There was no way out but straight ahead. "When I got to Millertons' with the cow, Abigale was gone, so I went looking for her." He left out the part about being mad as a hornet. "I fetched Pop's shotgun off the wall before I rode out."

"Thank God." Abigale's whisper skimmed the air, but Emmy caught it.

"Did you shoot something?" His sister's eyes were big as saucers.

"I shot *at* something. Scared it off."

"A mountain lion."

Abigale's comment sucked the air from the room.

Emmy got up from where she'd been playing with her dolls and hugged him. "That makes you a hero, Seth."

Then she gave Abigale an exaggerated wink. "Told ya so."

Abigale turned bright pink and buried her face in Chester's neck.

"Time for bed, little lady. Come on." Ma ushered Emmy and her dolls upstairs.

Pa added a couple of logs to the fire, then turned his back to the flames, hands stretched out behind him. "Good to have you with us, Abigale. I'm glad you're safe and sound."

"It's good to be here, Mr. Holt."

"Ben. Just Ben. Like Ida said, we're family."

Pride flickered behind his eyes and he gave Seth a quick nod. "Glad you found them in time, son." Then he took to the stairs.

Seth could have sliced the tension with a crosscut saw. It hadn't been like this at the Millerton place when it was only him and Abigale. He missed the ease of their company, there in the big log house alone, where he could take her in his arms and ask her to marry him without anybody other than Chester listening in.

Course he hadn't even come close to doing such a thing, but he'd thought about it enough.

Yeah, he missed those few special days.

He hoped he hadn't missed his opportunity as well.

CHAPTER 13

S now fell every day for a week. Abigale had never been completely alone in a heavy winter storm, and she was beyond grateful that she wasn't now.

Not that she wouldn't have done just as well at home by herself. She split wood and built fires and fed stock and did everything else that one did to survive. But that wasn't what mattered, what warmed her heart.

Seth and his family did that.

Her first morning with the Holts, she had helped Ida knead bread dough and chop vegetables for a stew. Ben Holt evidently ate as much as his son if the amount of food Ida prepared was any indication. Two iron kettles simmered at the back of the stove, and by dinner time, four loaves of fresh bread perfumed the air.

Emmy had churned sweet and salted butter, and Abigale helped her press it into molds. Ida's joy in serving her family far outshone anything Abigale had once considered pleasant at Wolfe Hall, and only drew her deeper into the high-country life she'd loved as a child.

The next week played out with the same routines. Similar to the way Mams's fine stitches framed her needlework, everyone's appointed chores framed the family. Abigale felt a part of it too, for she was not excluded from the daily labor as each person's help was needed and appreciated.

November blew into December, raising deeper drifts against the barn and anticipation in the house. The day Seth and his father dragged a cut pine through the door, Emmy nearly came apart with delight.

"A Christmas tree! A Christmas tree!" She clapped and hopped around her papa and brother like a little bird.

Seth winked at his sister and tweaked her nose, then gave Abigale a banked-coal look that sent her pulse racing not too awfully far ahead of her imagination.

Escaping upstairs to her room, she left the family to their traditions while she considered her predicament: no gifts to share at Christmas.

Already she'd learned from Emmy that Ben Holt read the Christ-child story every Christmas Eve after supper and the family exchanged presents.

As much as she adored her grandmother's needlework, Abigale didn't adore the effort it required. Handwork was a skill completely wasted on her, though Mams had never put it so cruelly. Abigale simply did not care to poke a needle and thread in and out of hooped cloth until a pretty picture resulted. She'd much rather ride, work in the garden, or read. But how did those things translate into Christmas gifts?

Her baked goods were always well received, but they seemed such a common thing at this time of year. Ida Holt's table was never anything less than heavily laden. What could Abigale possibly give this generous family they didn't already have?

Pushing the window curtain aside, she found the ranch and surrounding grasslands a Currier and Ives lithograph.

Such a snowy landscape was not a problem for ranchers who seldom drove into town, as had been her own custom for years. But she knew exactly what she wanted to give Seth, and now she couldn't get to it.

Her cheeks warmed merely thinking about the scarf in the glass-topped display case. How it would accentuate the meadow hue of his hazel eyes. Was such a gift too intimate, reserved only for wives and husbands, parents and children? Even so, she longed to see it on him and chided herself for letting anger blind her that day to the not-so-distant future.

If only she could ride to Briggs' mercantile and see if the neckerchief was still there.

Her sigh puffed against the windowpane. *If only* was an unprofitable consideration that did absolutely no good for anyone at all.

Retrieving Mams's receipt book from the bottom of a satchel, Abigale took it to the rocker and began searching for inspiration. Her grandmother's distinctive flourishes filled the pages, receipts for pies and cakes as well as potions and salves. As Abigale thumbed through the collection, a folded paper slid to the floor, one she'd forgotten about.

Another young woman from Wolfe Hall had shared her mother's receipt for peppermint pulls last year, warning that excessively humid air spoiled the endeavor. Humidity was typically no problem during a high-country winter, and this could be Abigale's answer. Only four ingredients were required, besides water, and with the sugar she'd brought, if Ida had peppermint extract, Abigale believed she could make the candy and divide it among the Holts. But she'd need to make a test batch or two in order to get it just right—and pray they didn't get a wet snow at the same time.

Folding the receipt, she stood and tucked it into her skirt pocket, encouraged by her plan—enthused, even, to find the sadness of Pop's absence tempered a bit with the prospect of giving.

The following day shone bright and clear, inspiring Ida to catch up on washing she had delayed. Abigale helped pin items on the drying lines and noticed Ben Holt saddling his horse at the barn.

She reached for the clothespins Emmy offered. "Where's your pa going?"

"He's riding in to Divide for something he ordered. I hope it's sugar sticks and new cloth for my doll clothes."

Abigale dropped the wooden pins in the muddy snow beneath her and stooped to help Emmy pick them up. "Sorry about that. If you go rinse these off inside, I'll take the bag and finish pinning."

Emmy bunched the dirty pins in her apron and headed for the house.

Abigale quickly finished with a tablecloth and worked her way around to Ida who was pinning clothes on the second of two strung lines.

"Nice day for a ride into town, isn't it?" Nonchalance was not Abigale's strong suit any more than pretending and lying. In fact, she was beginning to think she'd didn't have one, other than straight-forward opinion, so she simply blurted out what she wanted to say. "What takes your husband into town today?"

Ida appeared unoffended by Abigale's nosey question and kept right on pinning bloomers and petticoats. "He ordered a wagon part at the mercantile and wanted to take this warm spell to see if it arrived."

Oh dear. If Abigale hem-hawed around he'd be gone. "Do you think he'd mind picking up something for me as well?"

That stopped Ida's busy hands, and she gave Abigale her full attention. "Well, it depends on what it is. If he can carry it in a saddlebag, I'm sure he wouldn't mind. Go ask him, and I'll finish with these clothes."

Oh, for pity's sake. Abigale would rather walk to town than ask Seth's pa to check on the scarf for her, but this might be her last chance before Christmas. She handed the bag of pins to Ida. "Do you happen to have peppermint extract?"

Ida's expression brightened into a mischievous smile. "Sounds like you're in a candy-making mood. I don't have peppermint, and I'd be surprised if Mr. Briggs had any either. But you can ask Ben to check for you."

"Please—don't let him leave until I get back with the money."

"There's no need—"

Abigale didn't hear the rest, because she'd hiked her skirts and dashed up the back-porch steps and through the door, where she pulled her work boots off. Thank goodness she hadn't worn her lace-ups this morning.

In her room, she snatched her reticule, then raced back downstairs and into her boots. Ben sat astride his horse at the clothesline, and at her approach, gathered what looked like laughter and tucked it behind his knowing eyes.

Oh, the discomfort she went through for Seth Holt. This might be the most embarrassing thing she'd ever done on purpose.

"I hear you need peppermint extract," Ben said with thinly veiled humor.

Abigale emptied what money she had into her hand and placed it in his.

He frowned. "This is more than enough. Here." He offered most of it back to her.

She clasped her reticule in both hands and stepped back. "Well, there is one more thing—if you don't mind checking on something for me. I have no idea how much it is, but I'm hoping what I've given you is enough. If it isn't, then never mind. The peppermint will do."

Ben glanced at his wife, who patted his knee and looked up at him with nothing less than love.

He covered her hand and directed his question to Abigale. "What is it?"

A blush warmed her neck, but she didn't have all day. She gambled on the lifetime acquaintance of this loving family to keep them from thinking her improper. "When I was there last month, I saw a green silk neckerchief in Mr. Briggs's display case. Of course it might be gone by now, but if you don't mind, would you check and see? And if it's there, would you buy it for me, along with the peppermint? Providing I've given you enough money, of course."

He dropped Abigale's money in his coat pocket and tugged his hat down in a way that reminded her of Seth. "Anything else?"

"If there's money left over, I'd appreciate a length of ribbon too. Any color. And please, don't tell anyone about it."

His piercing gaze, so like his son's, sank her voice all the way to her toes. "The scarf, that is. I'd like it to be a surprise."

One side of his mouth quirked.

Ida covered a smile.

"I'll be back before supper." He leaned from the saddle and kissed his wife full on the mouth. Right in front of Abigale.

From the loft, Seth watched Abigale hand something to his pa and then step back clutching that little bag of hers. He'd bet his loaded pitchfork she had a scheme going.

When Pa leaned down and kissed his mother, Seth chuckled. He'd also bet that Abigale was blushing like a summer rose.

He pitched the hay over the edge of the loft into a wheelbarrow below, more than a little pleased that he'd finished patching Abigale's barn. The place needed a lot more work with Pop unable to carry the load the last couple of years. Seth wondered what Abigale planned to do come spring. All her stock had been sold off, other than what he'd driven home.

Most folks thought she'd sell out, and he'd been one of those folks until he'd heard otherwise. His world had brightened considerably because he knew there was more to Abigale Millerton's determination than mere talk, but he doubted she had money to start another herd. She couldn't tend her hayfields alone, and she'd need a crew to harvest her timber once they figured out what to do with Blackwell.

He snorted. Blackwell's *wife*. Sounded like the whole family was in on the pilfering, and Abigale couldn't take them on single-handedly. He intended to help whether she wanted him to or not, but it'd sure be a lot easier if she did. And he planned to do whatever it took to change her mind in the next couple of weeks.

That evening after supper, Emmy cajoled him into stringing popcorn and dried chokecherries. His ma and Abigale busied themselves making gingerbread men and sugar cookies for tree ornaments, and Pa cleaned a couple of rifles.

While Seth poked his fingers full of holes, the sweet smell of ginger and sugar churned up memories from his childhood. How he'd looked forward to Christmas Eve and what his ma had tucked into the tree for him. That particular anticipation had faded as he'd grown, and he figured he enjoyed her special baking more than anything else. Emmy kept them all on their toes with her wheedling and hinting at what she hoped for in her stocking. He'd long ago given up hanging a sock from the mantel. That was for youngsters.

Besides, what he wanted for Christmas wouldn't fit in a sock.

Well, one foot would.

He felt a smile tug his mouth as he recalled the stormy night he'd pulled wool socks onto Abigale's alabaster feet. He glanced into the kitchen and caught her watching him. She quickly looked back to her cutting board, but he'd seen something in her eye that made him shake on the inside.

Did she have feelings for him like he did for her?

"I heard some interesting news in town today." Pa wiped the barrel of his Winchester, deliberately stretching everyone's curiosity with a long silence, as was his custom.

"And?" Emmy hadn't learned to wait him out.

Pa stalled a minute more, then aimed the rifle up the staircase, thumbing an imaginary speck of dust off the sights.

"Don't be spreading gossip, Ben." Ma rolled her pin over a lump of cookie dough.

"Wouldn't dream of it, dear." He lowered the gun and, with a different rag, polished the wooden stock. "Briggs said Blackwell's son came in the mercantile last weekend and bought two axes."

"Ben." Ma's tone sharpened.

"Said the young man was a little shook up."

"Not the best topic for young ears, Ben."

Emmy rolled her eyes.

Pa flicked a glance at Seth. "Told Briggs someone had taken potshots at him in the woods."

A cookie sheet clattered to the kitchen floor and everyone jumped.

"Ow!" Seth jerked his hand and stuck the offended finger in his mouth.

"If you'd pay attention to what you're doing and stop watching Abigale, you wouldn't be so bloody." Emmy didn't duck because she knew he wouldn't box her ears in front of their pa.

"I'm so sorry." Abigale knelt to clean up the mess.

"Why don't you take a break while I salvage these fellas. A missing arm or two never hurt any gingerbread man I ever met."

Leave it to Ma to try to lighten the atmosphere, but this time it didn't work. Seth's steam was rising as fast as the blood beading on his finger.

"Thank you, Ida. I believe I'll go look in on Chester at the barn. See how he's doing." Abigale hung her apron over a chair and slid into Pop's old coat.

Seth laid his string of corn aside and went for his boots. "I'll go with you."

Abigale's phony smile might have fooled everyone else, but it didn't fool him.

"Oh, that won't be necessary. I'm only going to the barn. And it's not snowing."

"I wanna go—"

Pa jabbed Emmy in the arm and shook his head. She sulled up and went back to sewing corn on thread, but not before sticking her tongue out at Seth.

CHAPTER 14

Seth hoofed it to the barn in short order, the rope path melted down to mud in the last two days. He'd run out without a lantern—so had Abigale—but a half moon threw light on the yard, and he knew the inside of the barn like he knew the inside of his boot with his eyes closed. He grabbed a lantern there and soon had it lighting the alleyway and box stalls. One stood open.

Abigale sat beside Chester, knees to her chest, the dog's shaggy tail sweeping the straw. The ranch dogs looked up at Seth's arrival, drawing Abigale's attention as well.

He could see her stiffen.

How could he be so churned up inside over a gal who made him crazy with her bull-headed, independent, do-as-she-pleased ways?

He hung the lantern on a nail and stepped into the stall. "You told me you didn't go up there to—"

"I don't answer to you, Seth Holt."

"Both names, is it now? Next thing I know, you'll be calling me *Mr.* Holt." This wasn't going well, but hang it all, didn't she know she was putting herself in danger?

He crossed one foot over the other and sank to the straw beside her.

"How do you do that?" Anger buck-stitched her every word.

"How do you do *that*?"

She scowled. "Do what?"

"Flip everything over like a pile of flapjacks. I'm the one with the right to be mad and you're bringing up how I sit."

"You do *not* have a right to be mad. Why do you challenge everything I want to do?"

"I don't challenge everything you want to do. Except when I know you could get hurt."

With a hand against the wall, she pushed to her feet. "There you go again—when you *know*. As if I don't know anything or can't do anything on my own."

In a single easy move, he stood and took a step toward her.

She backed up, apprehension washing her face in the dim light.

"I'm tired of arguing with you, Abigale, so why don't you just marry me?"

Not the best way of going about things, but the woman made him loco.

She shoved her hands against her hips and pitched her chin at him. "So you can boss me around even more? You think just because we're married you can tell me what to do?"

"We're not married. Not yet, anyway. And no, that's not why I want to marry you."

She gave him a side-eyed look, like a jittery colt watchin' a man move in with a halter. "So why, then?"

He took another step, slower. Reached out and pushed her braid over her shoulder, then ran his hands down her arms, gentle-like, until the tension in them eased.

She blinked, and her breath came warm against his face as he lowered his mouth to hers. Her hands slid around his waist and pressed into his back.

Wrapping her in his arms, he kissed her until he thought he'd never breathe again, then raised his head and whispered against her hair. "Because I care about you, Aspen-gal. I always have. Let me love you."

~

Abigale opened her mouth to answer, but she couldn't. She couldn't hear anything but Seth's heartbeat in her ear. Couldn't feel anything but the warm strength of his embrace. Everyone she'd ever loved had been taken from her. How could she risk losing him too?

At her silence, his arms loosened and a disappointed sigh leaked from his chest.

She stepped back and, in spite of her coat, instantly chilled, forcing her to hug herself instead of him.

Chester rose and nuzzled her leg with a whine, sensing her distress.

"Don't stay out here long." Seth's voice dropped and his throaty words scratched her heart. "I mean—I'll walk you back if you want."

She shook her head, unable to answer or even look at him. A tear escaped and she caught it with her finger. Fine time to spring a leak.

Without another sound, he walked out, leaving the lantern behind. Always thinking of her welfare. Always loyal. Always kind.

No. More than kind. Images from over the years flashed through her memory like summer lightning—his caring ways, his protection. *His love.* Finally seeing it for what it was, her tears rose anew.

Let me love you. He hadn't even demanded her love in return.

When she was certain he'd left the barn, she fell to the straw, wrapped her arms around Chester, and wept into the dog's thick winter coat.

~

Abigale didn't know how long she'd stayed in the barn, but the moon had slid behind its peaked roof by the time she left. Grateful for the lantern, she let its yellow wash guide her until she reached the porch. Extinguishing the flame, she set the lantern on a small table beside Ida's rocker. So many summers, during carefree days, the woman had sat there mending clothes or stringing beans or enjoying a glass of lemonade. Such a homey scene, one that Abigale had longed for and yet ...

She eased the front door open and hung Pop's coat on the rack. Seth's was there, and relief slipped out on a breath. He was inside, safe, and not riding through a snowy field in the dark.

Upstairs, Abigale fell across the bed without undressing and drew the quilt around her, tucking her chin beneath it. The words on her grandmother's pillow top stitched through her mind. *Trust in the Lord, and do good.*

"I'm scared, Lord. Scared of someday losing Seth if I let him love me. Scared of losing him now if I don't. Show me what to do." Her whisper lifted only as high as the quilt covering her mouth, and sleep overcame her before she could ask more.

A tapping on glass woke her, and wrapped in the quilt, she padded to the window. Daylight fought for purchase, but an icy sleet held sway, clattering against the pane. She shivered.

Halfway down the stairs, she met the enticing aroma of strong coffee. A fire burned full and bright on the hearth, and Ida's warm voice from the kitchen joined its invitation.

"You're up early this morning."

Not seeing a cup on the table, Abigale took two from the hutch and filled them with coffee, offering one to Ida.

"Thank you, dear." Her worried glance swept Abigale's disheveled state. "Did you not sleep well?"

"I guess not." She tucked loosened hair behind her ears, embarrassed that she hadn't even bothered to brush it. Tempted to pour her heart out as liberally as she spooned sugar into her coffee, she swallowed her jumbled feelings and drowned them with the hot brew.

Ida joined her at the table and retrieved a flat package from her apron pocket, wrapped in brown mercantile paper and cross-tied with a double length of pink ribbon. She pushed it across the table and followed it with a small brown bottle of peppermint extract. "Ben brought these for you, but I didn't get a chance to give them to you yesterday."

As if they had never dried, fresh tears rose. Abigale swiped at them unsuccessfully until Ida offered her a folded towel.

"I'm s-sorry." Her stuttered breath embarrassed her as much as her hair.

"I'm a good listener, Abigale. If there's anything you want to say, I'm right here. I might not have all the answers, but I do know that a broken gingerbread man goes nicely with hot coffee and a broken heart."

Unable to look her hostess in the eyes, Abigale squeezed her own tightly shut. What was the matter with her? She'd never acted so cowardly, nor backed down from confrontation so quickly.

Maybe that was the problem. This was not confrontational, nor was Seth's embrace and kiss last night.

When Ida rose for the plate of cookies, Abigale slipped the narrow grosgrain from the package. Inside, the beautiful green silk shimmered in the kitchen lamp's glow, and she pushed it away from her, afraid to stain it with her tears.

Ida set the plate between them and chose a broken man. "Is it not what you wanted?"

"No, it's perfect. It's exactly what I wanted."

Steeped in the sanctuary of home, Ida's voice softened. "Then why do you push it away?"

Abigale heard the unspoken question, one that addressed what had happened in the barn. She *did* love Seth, and she wanted to let him love her, as he put it, but her fear pushed him away.

"If I may be so bold, Abigale, I take it things did not go well with … *Chester* last night."

A painfully weak smiled escaped, and Abigale dunked her cookie, bit off a coffee-soaked leg, and shook her head.

"I surmised as much by the racket Seth made stomping up the stairs and shoving things around in his room till all hours." Understanding softened the curve of her mouth. "Is there someone in Denver?"

Abigale shook her head again. She'd met upstanding, ambitious young men, but none of them appealed to her with their city suits and formal ways.

"Seth can be as opinionated as his father, I'm afraid. But only when it involves something—or someone—he cares dearly for." Ida reached across the table for the scarf and fingered the fine jacquard silk. "This is beautiful, and capable of warming the wearer during this high country's coldest days."

"I wanted to give it to Seth for Christmas."

"Really."

Heavy with a sense of knowing, the single word was not a question.

"You say *wanted.* Did something happen to make you change your mind?"

Abigale's grip on the damp towel eased, as did her hold on her emotions. Where else could she pour out her doubts?

"I've lost everyone I've ever loved. Everyone who ever cared about me. If I love Seth"—she glanced at his mother—"I might lose him too. I couldn't bear it."

Ida took another cookie and dunked the head in her coffee. "May I ask you a personal question?"

With nothing to gain by refusing, Abigale nodded.

"How would you have felt after your grandparents died if you'd never told them you loved them? If you'd never returned their affection?"

The question hit her like a stinging wasp, and she stared at her hostess, stunned by the woman's directness.

"Would it have made their passing easier to bear?"

The ache of her grandparents' absence throbbed, stealing most of her voice. "No. It would have made things much worse, much emptier."

"That's the way of love, dear. Seth has loved you since before he knew what it meant for a man to love a woman." Ida picked up the brown bottle and smoothed a wrinkle in the tablecloth before replacing it. "And I believe you've had feelings for him nearly as long. It may be more difficult for you to see, because you are looking at things from the inside out. But to the rest of us, it is quite clear."

Almost as an afterthought to herself she added, "Sometimes we no longer see what's become familiar."

So like what Seth had told her on their way to town that day. *It's easy to take for granted what we're used to.*

Gentle laughter raised Abigale's gaze. "The two of you also bicker like siblings because you grew up together. Ben and I were much the same before we married, having both lived in this valley."

Her countenance misted over with memories, and she spooned out the cookie piece that had sunk to the bottom of her cup. "Once I saw myself and Ben as complementing each other instead of competing—adding to, not taking away—and building up rather than tearing down, things changed for the better."

Abigale wiped her fingers on the towel and picked up the scarf, letting it spill like a green waterfall on the table. It was big enough for Seth to wrap around his throat twice, as ranchers did.

"He asked me to marry him last night. Well—in a way. He didn't really *ask*. It was closer to *telling*."

"And you didn't take that well, did you." Ida chuckled and sipped her crumb-filled coffee. "Nor should you. Never let him ride roughshod over you, but neither forget that he loves you. It will make all the difference in your partnership. If you choose to marry him, that is."

"Mams would have said to have faith."

"And she'd be right. Faith is something we carry with us. Trust, on the other hand, is something we do. The two work together, like the light and darker weave in that jacquard-patterned scarf."

Ida gave Abigale's hand a gentle squeeze. "I won't tell you to follow your heart. But I will tell you that God gives us faith so we can trust Him. He'll let you know. All you have to do is ask."

CHAPTER 15

"Technically, I asked her."

Seth pulled the curry comb through Coop's tail, then moved to his shoulder and worked back. He hadn't ridden the gelding in the last couple of days, and Coop's heavy winter coat needed a good brushing.

"All right. Maybe not. It wasn't the most poetic proposal known to man, but I'm not some high-collared gent she'd meet in Denver."

Coop bobbed his head as if in agreement. Seth ran the comb down his back, and the flesh quivered in response.

After finishing the left side, he moved around to the right, continuing along Coop's body and upper legs, then removed the long tail hair from the comb, dislodging the short thicker hair with it. He brushed the horse, checked each hoof, and rewarded Coop's good nature with a can of oats.

Seth had worn a groove in his brain, deep as a wagon rut going over what he'd said to Abigale last night in the barn. He'd shown his hand, and he didn't know what to say different now. He loved her and thought he'd told her so.

But she'd pulled away.

Coop looked at him over the stall and tossed his head. For no good reason. Same thing he'd done when Seth was training him as a colt.

He did it again and blew, then went back to the oats. The mannerism was something Seth'd had to figure out. It'd taken him a while, but he was no quitter, and he eventually won the gelding over.

If he'd given up, he wouldn't have the fine horse he had today. The working relationship they had. The mutual trust and companionship.

Some things were worth repeating until you got them right.

He reached over the stall and patted Coop's neck. "You're a good man, Cooper Brown."

"Did you just call your horse a man?"

More than the surprise of her showing up, the challenge in Abigale's tone tilted Seth's heart toward hope. Where there was a spark, there was chance of a flame.

Keeping a tight rein on anticipation, he turned and faced her.

She was different somehow. Just as pretty, just as bold, but there was a softness around her eyes as she handed him a small bundle.

"These are from, uh, your mother. She thought you might be hungry."

Abigale always had been a horrible liar.

"Thank you—I mean, her. Thank her for me." He unfolded the napkin and found a gingerbread man with a frosted smile. The cookie beneath it had been cut differently, without legs, but what looked like a skirt. He met Abigale's gaze as she read his reaction.

She crossed her arms and glanced away. "We've been experimenting."

The cookies were still warm. "Want a bite? I'll share."

"No, they're for you. I—your mother—wanted you to have them. There are plenty more inside."

He finished off the first one. "No milk?"

Her fists shot to her hips, her eyes narrowed. "Seth Holt, you ungrateful, incorrigible—"

One step took him to her, close enough to smell flour and cinnamon on her clothes. Close enough that her skirt brushed his leg and his boot clipped the edge of hers.

She didn't back away.

He gentled his voice, resisting the urge to trail his fingers along her lovely neck. "You say there are others where these came from?"

She looked up at him with more than cookies on her mind, that much he knew for certain.

"Yes." Her hands dropped from her waist, and she pressed one against his chest, pinning him like a nail through a horseshoe. Quiet-like, as if she was telling him a secret, she raised up on her toes and her breath danced against his ear. "All you have to do is ask."

~

Christmas Eve arrived as frozen and lustrous as Abigale had found Aspen Falls, sheathed in a crystalline snow that kept Seth and his father parading from the wood pile to the back porch.

But the smells circling the kitchen were enough to warm her from the inside out. Turkey and dressing, pot roast and gravy. Pies—pumpkin, canned cherry, and mincemeat—and crocks full of cookies.

Her peppermint-candy pull had succeeded on her first attempt, so she'd made a second batch just for fun, resulting in a tidy bundle of twisted white canes for everyone in the family. In each length of ribbon securing the candy, she tucked a sprig of blue spruce harvested from the windbreak that hedged the ranch. The festive appearance pleased her immensely.

Almost as much as Seth's reaction to her peace offering.

There was no way of knowing if he'd understood her unspoken message with the gingerbread man and lady. But there was no doubting the hammer of his heart beneath her hand when she'd whispered in his ear.

Heat to rival Ida's cookstove shot through Abigale every time she thought about it. Which was nearly every minute and the main reason she'd opened the collar of her blouse and rolled up her sleeves.

Preparations were completed, the tree decorated, and the table set with Ida's best dishes. Emmy poked at packages until her mother set her to sorting buttons from an old jar.

Dinner was planned for near two o'clock, and wood was stacked on the back porch to last through the night. Seth and his father had made themselves scarce, and Abigale rejoiced in that small mercy. In the last few days, her hesitancy to love Seth had reverted to her earlier impulse to fling herself into his arms. Especially since she knew what those arms felt like.

Abigale stole away to her room, where she could work on her gifts. From the brown paper wrapping the scarf had come in, she cut fanciful shapes and tied one to each ribboned bundle of candy, labeling them with the recipient's name and a verse she thought appropriate for the person.

Her own verse played through her thoughts, impressed there as permanently as Mams's fine stitches on the pillow. *Trust in the Lord, and do good.*

Ida's remarks about faith and trust had shed new light on the familiar phrase, particularly the little word Abigale had so often skipped over. Somehow, it now made a world of difference.

She wrapped Seth's candy with the remaining paper and then the silk scarf before sliding it into one of the woolen socks he'd used the night he'd found her. That night seemed so long ago now, though it had been merely weeks.

Oddly enough, she'd been able to find only one sock, and when she asked Emmy if she'd seen the other, the girl merely looked away and shrugged.

After freshening herself, doing up her hair with a sprig of spruce and donning a lighter-weight but appropriate dress, she slipped downstairs and tucked her gifts into the tree branches. The fireplace mantel was dressed with pine cones and aromatic evergreen boughs, and she hung Seth's sock next to Emmy's.

When the family finally gathered at the table, Abigale noted that each person had dressed for the occasion. The men were freshly shaved and wearing clean shirts, and Emmy and Ida wore pinafore aprons over their dresses and high color in their cheeks. The meal was as delicious as anticipated, and by the time everyone had finished dessert and moved to sit by the fire, Abigale felt as giddy as Emmy. Her gaze strayed repeatedly to Seth, who seemed to watch her nearly as much as she watched him. She chose a chair easily moved and scooted it as far from the fire as possible without appearing rude to the people who had so generously welcomed her into their home.

Ben Holt took his place near the hearth and opened his Bible. Emmy propped her dolls around her where she sat on the floor, and Ida folded her hands in her aproned lap. Seth could have been standing on his head for all Abigale knew, because she refused to look at his handsome face. The flinging impulse might be more than she could resist.

Ben cleared his throat. "'And it came to pass in those days ...'"

Pop's tradition had been similar, reading from the second chapter of Luke, though he did so on Christmas morning. Bittersweet memories laced through Abigale, and she looked at each one before tying them off and tucking them away.

"'And so it was, that while they were there, the days were accomplished that she should be delivered ...'"

Abigale considered, perhaps for the first time, the double meaning of the word *delivered*. As a woman, and a ranching woman at that, she had a clear understanding of what the Scripture was saying. Birth. New life. A fresh start with a high-priced risk. But this year the word struck her differently, for she had been delivered from deep sadness, loneliness, and fear.

"Jesus was born in a barn." Emmy's commentary brought a smile to Ida's lips and raised her father's eyebrows at her interruption.

Ida's hand on her daughter's shoulder appeared to comfort and encourage Emmy at the same time. The woman had a gift for that, and Abigale thought again of her pointed question regarding Mams and Pop. The barb had dulled with perspective, for Abigale had seen that one did not protect herself from loss by refusing to give love.

"'And the angel said to them, "Fear not: for, behold, I bring you good tidings of great joy, which shall be to all people. For unto you is born this day in the city of David a Savior, which is Christ, the Lord.""'"

Emmy leaned over her dolls and whispered loudly, "They put him in the feed trough."

Ben finished the chapter, and everyone bowed their heads, so Abigale followed suit.

"We thank You again, Lord, for the gift of Your son, Jesus, and for Your love. We thank You for Your provision throughout the year, our safe herds, this home, and our family. And we thank You for sending Abigale to us this year to celebrate Christ's birth. Amen."

Abigale quickly swiped at her eyes before everyone's responsive *amen.*

Emmy sprang up, dislodging her dolls, and dug into the presents tucked in and around the tree. Ida rose and headed for the kitchen. Abigale stood to follow her, but a warm hand to her arm paused her progress.

"You stay here, Abigale. It's only hot cocoa and cookies I'm passing out. I want you to relax and enjoy the moment."

Abigale had known Ida Holt long enough to know that her word ruled in the kitchen, so she smiled her thanks and took her seat.

In mere minutes, everyone had a pile of small gifts on their lap, and Emmy was wriggling beneath the tree and out again with a woolen sock. *The* woolen sock for which Abigale had searched. With an imp-like glimmer in her eye, she laid it in Abigale's lap.

Abigale glanced around to make certain all the gifts were distributed, then pointed Emmy toward the sock on the mantel and indicated she give it to Seth.

"Why, it's just like the sock I gave you." The girl glanced between Abigale and her brother.

Ida had returned with a tray of steaming mugs and cookies, and she and Ben exchanged a knowing look. Everyone was glancing about, a most comical situation, Abigale thought, except for Seth who looked as nervous as she'd felt during her entrance exam at Wolfe Hall, afraid she'd disappoint her grandparents by not being accept—

She squeezed the sock in her lap, seemingly empty, until she came to a small lump in the toe.

Every eye in the room rested on her, but she refused to be the center of attention. "Please, open your gifts. I cannot wait to see what you each received."

Emmy needed no more encouragement and squealed with delight at the lovely doll dresses from her parents and the new bridle from Seth. Each person thanked Abigale for their *personal* bundle of peppermint sticks, and Emmy begged the ribbons from Ben and Ida's candy to use in her dolls' hair.

Seth's gaze held Abigale in place, and she feared he would stare a hole all the way through her, discovering all her secrets while he was at it.

In truth, she had very few secrets he didn't already know about, but one glimmered so brightly she felt he must see it in her eyes.

CHAPTER 16

When Seth's calloused fingers hit silk, he knew what the sock held. Only one thing felt so fine, other than Abigale's lips against his own.

But the quality of the moss-green scarf set him back. He unfolded the large square, its paisley pattern contrasting light against dark, but all in the same soft green. Feeling Abigale's eyes on him, he looked up to find her brimming with expectation.

Slowly, he doubled the scarf at opposite corners, laid it against his throat, and crossed the ends behind his neck. Then watching her all the while, he brought the corners back around and tied them in a flat knot known to cattlemen and cowboys.

Her lips curved in a soft smile.

"Thank you," he mouthed across the noisy room.

She smiled more fully, pleased by his pleasure.

He nodded toward the matching wool sock she held.

Uncertainty clouded her features, and his heart lurched to his throat. But when she reached inside and stopped short, he crossed the room and dropped in his customary fashion to sit at her feet.

"Abigale Rebecca Millerton, you're the most beautiful, frustrating, determined, take-my-breath-away woman I've ever met. You've had my heart since you insisted on shimmying down the wrong side of Aspen Falls and I thought I'd lose you."

A small laugh escaped, and her hands trembled as she drew out the cotton handkerchief edged with tiny blue forget-me-nots, corners gathered in a knot around his hopes.

He covered her hands with his and pushed up to one knee. "Will you be a rancher's wife? This cowboy's bride? Will you marry me and share my home and let me share your dreams?"

Her eyes shimmered and she blinked. "Why, Seth Leopold Holt, you *do* have a poet's heart. And yes, I will marry you. On one condition."

Air fled the room, not to mention his lungs, and at what must have been his stunned expression, she laid her hand against his cheek and leaned over until they were eye to eye.

"If you teach me how to sit down like you do in one fluid motion."

In spite of his family looking on, he kissed her. Right there on the mouth in front of the good Lord and his little sister. Then he drew back just enough to whisper, "Deal."

Realizing she hadn't opened her gift, he dropped back to the floor. "Go ahead. Finish."

She untied the loose knot and gasped at what lay tucked inside.

He picked up the finely etched gold band and lifted her left hand. "This was my grandmother's ring. I'd be honored if you'd be the next Holt woman to wear it." Pausing, he looked into her eyes. "Will you?"

She puddled up but his hands were full, and he couldn't wipe the tears from her cheeks.

EPILOGUE

Following the first Sunday service in January, Abigale stood at the back of Divide's small church, clutching a "bouquet" of young blue spruce and lodgepole pine sprigs, tied with the handkerchief Seth had given her the week before. His grandmother had carried the delicately trimmed hankie at her wedding, Ida had told her, and Abigale had marveled at the words stitched into its center.

My times are in Thy hand.

Nothing could have been more fitting.

And nothing encouraged her more for dealing with the Blackwell's pilfering come spring. Pop had often said a three-fold cord was stronger than any other, and she, Seth, and the Lord made three.

Ida had accompanied her to her grandparents' ranch to collect a blue dress Abigale saved for special occasions and her good button-top shoes. And this morning, she'd seated Abigale before her dressing table as she did up her hair with surprising dexterity. The girls at Wolfe Hall would be stunned that a high-country rancher's wife had such skill.

"I can read, you know," Ida had spouted when pressed about her ability. "*Godey's* and a few other magazines offer fine instructions as well as illustrations."

"Emmy is blessed to have you," Abigale said.

A final pin slipped into place, and Ida patted Abigale's shoulders. "And we are blessed to have you."

Movement at the front of the church drew Abigale's nervous attention back to the moment. The pastor signaled the piano player. Seth rose from the first pew and turned to face her. The green scarf was tied proudly at his throat and his best shirt fit snugly over his broad shoulders.

He had asked to borrow the ring for the ceremony, and she'd gladly slipped it on his little finger.

"I love you, Abigale," he'd said, kissing her with a tender passion that shivered all the way down to her toes.

Seth Holt had been surprising her most of her life, doing or saying the unexpected, and she had no doubt he would continue to do so.

There was that little word again. The word she longed to say once she reached the front of the church and stood before all the parishioners who had stayed to wish her well. Mams had stitched the word years ago, but only lately had Abigale realized its significance.

"I *do* trust You," she whispered on her way to stand beside her handsome, rough-cut cowboy.

And when the moment came, she looked into his meadow-green eyes and said it again out loud. "I do. With all my heart, I do."

~ ~ ~

Thank you for reading Seth and Abigale's story.
I would so appreciate a brief review on your favorite book
sites and/or social media.
Reviews help me reach other readers like you.

And thank you for allowing me literary license regarding
the great little community of Divide, Colorado – not quite
as developed in 1875 as I have depicted it in my story, but a
unique high-country town that survived and thrives today.

Continue reading for the second High-Country Christmas
novella, Snow Angel.

Snow Angel

Bless the LORD, ye his angels, that excel in strength, that do his commandments, hearkening unto the voice of his word.

Psalm 103:20

PROLOGUE

December 1864
Piney Hill, Colorado Territory

Lena pushed up the latch, slipped out the cabin door, and dashed down the front porch steps into the snow. Her brother thought he was so big because he was ten and had *grown-up* chores. Well, she didn't need him. She was big enough to make snow angels alone. A whole field of them. Rows and rows, like all the people at church on Sunday.

Ahead of her, the pasture gate sagged open. She ran toward it, pushing through snow that inched above her high-topped shoes until one stuck and she fell to her hands and knees. Icy pin pricks stung all the way to her elbows, but she shook her arms and bent her fingers open and closed, open and closed, their pink tips like rosebuds against the white ground. She'd forgotten her mittens and coat.

Never mind it. If she went back now, Tay would call her a baby. But she was no baby, she was four. She'd show him.

Crack! The chock of an ax chased over the snowy field, all the way from where Tay split firewood behind the cabin.

If only she could fly, there'd be no footprints following her. Wouldn't that be lovely? To fly like a bird, or a real angel with white wings and a shiny robe?

Twisting her fingers into her skirt, she trudged on to the gate, then squeezed through its open mouth at the fence post.

Behind her now, far away, smoke curled from their cabin chimney, thin and silvery like ribbon on a Christmas gift.

Would Christmas ever come? Papa said it would be here soon, but *soon* took forever.

The pasture lay perfectly still beneath its big white blanket, just like she did beneath her quilt when she pretended to sleep. No cows or birds or Sir Humphrey were there to muss it. Sir Humphrey was behind the cabin with Tay and she was glad. He liked to plow through the snow with his cold black nose and giant paws. He'd plow right through her field of angels.

A million tiny stars sparkled up from the ground, so bright it made her eyes hurt. Papa said the stars were crystals. Crystal would be a lovely name for the doll she wanted for Christmas. If she got a doll, she'd call it Crystal.

Spreading her arms wide, she faced the fence line, squeezed her eyes shut, and fell straight back. The dry snow caught her like a cloud of goose down, and she swept her arms up beside her head and down again, her legs out and together. Out and together. Then she stood and jumped as far as she could to a fresh spot and fell back again, swishing her arms and legs in the thick white powder. No footprints! Tay would wonder how she did it.

After a thousand angels, she lay still, breathing hard and puffing out clouds. The sky wasn't blue, but gray like the chimney smoke. Snowflakes tickled her face.

Pushing to her feet, she looked around. The cabin was gone, the gate too. Only the snowy ground and falling sky. Far, far away, in a high, tiny voice, Mama called.

"*Lee*-na! An-ge-*li*-na!"

Her stomach squeezed. She was in trouble now.

She had nothing to help her find her way home like Hansel and Gretel did—nothing but her field full of angels. They would lead her.

With a big swing of her arms, she jumped into the snow angel just before the last one she'd made. Then she jumped to the next one and the next one, forever and forever, until she came to the first one she'd made in front of the gate. She almost didn't see the tired old gate for the snow falling.

Cold pinched her nose and her toes, and her legs ached from jumping into a thousand angels. Maybe she could rest for a minute.

But Papa said never rest in the snow. Keep moving.

She pushed through the gap between the gate and the post and followed the fence line until it got lost in the trees. Icy air slipped in through her mouth and made her chest hurt. Her fingers burned, and she tucked them under her arms.

If she took a little rest—there, beneath that scraggly berry bush—only for a minute, Papa didn't have to know.

Branches scratched her head and plucked her hair as she crawled under the bush. The snow wasn't as deep, and she curled into a ball like Sir Humphrey did at night in front of the hearth.

"Stay open, eyes. You do what I say, now."

But they didn't do what she said, and it was warmer with them closed. She pretended she was home in the loft, in her own bed where her fingers wouldn't hurt so badly. She curled tighter, pretending she was a dog like Sir Humphrey.

Something pulled her out from under the bush, and she pulled at her eyelids, trying to get them open. Strong arms wrapped around her and lifted her up so high she felt like she really was flying. She wasn't afraid, and her mouth wanted to smile, but it was pressed against a furry coat like Sir Humphrey's, only thicker. Warmer. She snuggled into it and it began moving, trudging through the snow like Papa. But it wasn't Papa. He would have scolded her and kissed her on the top of her head.

Long slow steps crunched through the snow until they climbed the porch and went inside the cabin. Cedar logs crackled on the fire, and the smell of supper soup filled up the air around her.

Down, down she eased against a quilt, and her eyes finally did what she told them and opened.

He wore a thick brown coat like a big bear. A fur cap covered his head and ears, and his face had a light inside it, like a lamp shining behind a curtain. He smiled, and it made her feel sleepy and safe and cozy all at the same time. But what she noticed most were his eyes—blue crystals. They smiled too, with little lines spreading out at the corners.

And when he stood, he was bigger than Papa. Too big for their tiny cabin, but somehow he fit inside without bumping his head.

He added a log to the fire and leaned so close she thought his cap would singe. The flames jumped up bright and shining, but they didn't burn him or his fur hat.

When he left, he closed the door so quietly she didn't hear a thing. Not a thing—other than Mama and Papa yelling her name outside. Even Tay yelled her whole name, not just *Lee* like he usually did.

Sir Humphrey barked and scratched at the door. She should let him in, but she couldn't force herself off Mama and Papa's bed.

Supper would be soon.

And the fire was so warm, the quilt so soft.

She snuggled deeper. Squeezed her eyes shut and saw again the light of the stranger's crinkly smile.

CHAPTER 1

October 1884
Piney Hill, Colorado

C innamon. Cloves. *Oranges*, for heaven's sake. A heady perfume with a hefty price.

Lena mentally tallied her purchases. Such indulgence. But Christmas came only once in twelve months, and if she spread her extravagance out over the next eight weeks, they could manage.

She thanked Mr. Fielding at the mercantile and headed home, a quarter-of-a-mile trip in good weather. Today it felt farther. The sky hung low, goose gray, and promising rain, which meant mud. It should be snowing this time of year, with the cottonwoods flashing yellow along the road, their aspen cousins trickling gold down the hillside at the end of town.

Smelling the storm's approach, she hiked her skirt and quickened her pace.

The one thing she could count on *this time of year* was her heart flip-flopping between cherished memories and painful recollections. Between excitement and dread.

Anticipation swept her along when she was shopping or planning meals or decorating cookies for the children at church. But at night, while cleaning up supper dishes after

Tay went to bed, apprehension hung like stubborn cobwebs in the corners of the dim kitchen. Fear that a horribly painful accident would happen again.

And she'd lose something else.

A fat rain drop hit her shoulder, and pain shuddered down her left arm to her hand. She cradled it protectively against her waist as she crossed the yard and climbed the porch steps. Lord, would this seasonal sensitivity never end? Twenty years. Twenty years was enough!

After dressing the hall tree with her cloak and hat, she took her bag of spices and fruit to the kitchen. Nothing was going to change. God help her, when would she accept that?

An hour later, the front door crashed inward.

Lena scrubbed her hands on her apron and ran down the hall.

Tay was dragging a man into the surgery, and two muddy feet trailed over the threshold, toes up. One booted, one bare.

As she reached to close the front door, a gray sharp-eared dog darted through.

"Grab his legs." Tay's voice hardened with urgency. "Be careful with the left one. Fibula's broken and the ankle's dislocated."

As usual, he excelled at overstating the obvious.

The rag-doll man hung limp, head lolling as Tay lined him up with the narrow surgery table. She stepped between the mismatched feet, linked her left arm around the right leg, and grabbed a fistful of woolen trouser on the other. Careful not to bump the bare foot that flopped at an unnatural angle.

"On three," Tay said. "One, two, *three*!"

The poor fellow landed on the table with a thud, and his dog uttered a near-human groan. Just so it didn't bite. She had enough to think about with its owner's legs hanging off the end of the table, perfectly even with the broken bone.

"Hold him and I'll get the board."

As if she could.

Ignoring the dog, Tay bolted through the door, down the hall, and out the back door. Headed for the barn, she knew, where he'd been working on an extension for his table. Last week, Joseph Cooper and his mangled arm had also been too long. Tay had to figure out a solution or order a new table.

Lena wrinkled her nose at the mix of muddy clothing and wet dog hair. Standing between the stranger's feet, she gently lowered the booted one to more steadily hold the other with both hands. Her starched apron was soiled now, but that was easily corrected. Much easier than setting this man's bones end on end and securing them that way.

His left arm dangled over the edge of the table, and the dog stood directly beneath it, watching her from between long, still fingers. One eye was honey-colored, the other like a blue opal, both challenging her to shoo it away.

She dared not. Holding the foot upright and praying the man didn't come to was challenge enough.

Footsteps hammered down the hall, and Tay rushed in holding a wide, thin board. He aimed it toward her end of the table, and she lifted the crooked leg higher.

The man moaned.

"His weight should counter-balance the board and keep it on the table." In spite of October's early chill, sweat trickled from Tay's tawny hairline and slid in rivulets down his temples.

Wedging the board beneath his patient, he pushed it, then lifted the right leg onto the board and pushed some more. "All right, ease that leg down."

Like a tongue worrying a broken tooth, her eyes kept returning to the crooked foot. She'd force them away and they'd whip right back, curiosity overruling her tumbling stomach.

She tried again, tacking her gaze to the man's dark matted hair and roughening beard. "You need a longer table."

"We can't afford it."

"If people paid you with real money, we could."

Tay shot her a we've-been-over-this-before scowl and gave the board a final shove. They tugged a clean sheet beneath the man, covering the board.

Tay rolled up his sleeves. "Take off his trousers and I'll wash up."

Hers was always the indelicate work.

Regardless of a patient's gender or injury, the appearance of rarely seen skin startled her every time, aside from Cecilia Valdez. The dressmaker had somehow stabbed herself with a pair of scissors last year and hadn't the stomach to stitch up the wound. Lena didn't blame her.

Most people's covered flesh was startlingly pale beneath their clothes and smooth as a baby's belly. Cecilia's skin had been rich and satiny like rolled-out gingerbread dough.

This stranger was most people.

But for the dark hair on his shins, his lower legs were white as boiled chicken, as was his brow, where a hat must have spent most of its time. His sun-browned face and hands more closely matched his boot leather than his body.

Lena tossed his trousers and single sock to the corner where she collected soiled sheets and bandages. Then, hands on her hips, she assessed his faded under-flannel.

Well worn, and a bit short, as if he'd grown out of them. But he was too old to have grown that much lately. His chin whiskers indicated more than twenty years, but not enough to salt his muddy mop with white strands.

As far as she could tell, he had no leg injuries above the knees, so that was where she made the first cut. At the knee. And then the other. No point in having mismatched drawers.

His was not the first broken bone she'd helped Tay set, but it was the most challenging. Bunched muscles and tight tendons fought against her as she wrestled with his pale foot, flinching each time it twisted to the side. She braced one foot against a chair wedged under the makeshift extension, wrapped her left arm around his right ankle, and gripped the bare foot with her other hand.

But when Tay pulled from the man's shoulders, the entire man moved—broken leg, crooked foot, and all.

Tay growled his frustration but wouldn't look at her. He never blamed her for her inadequacies, and sometimes she wished he would. His failure to address the issue was tantamount to ignoring a bison standing square in the center of the room.

"I have an idea," she said.

Tay closed his eyes and rubbed the sides of his head, frustration clear in his clenched jaw.

"You could loop one end of a rope around his chest and under his arms, then run the other end out the window, and tie it around Winnie's neck."

Tay's shock alone was worth the suggestion, except she knew it would work.

"Winnie could jerk him right through the window!"

Lena sucked in one cheek, the side her brother couldn't see, and bit off a snort. "Not if I hold her head and you pull his leg into place from this end, then holler when you're finished."

Tay frowned at his patient.

"Or we can keep this up until he wakes from the pain."

The frown dissipated, and her brother's jaw shifted sideways in surrender.

CHAPTER 2

L ena opened the oven door, hooked the iron kettle handle with a finger, and with a quilted hot pad, scooted the beans inside. They'd be done in time for a late supper.

So would Tay.

His recent Good Samaritan act had set him back on his rounds about four hours. But he'd always considered time a well-spent commodity, not something to be pinched.

He'd splinted the man's leg, then held him upright from the waist while she bathed and salved his ravaged back and shoulders. Though unconscious and relaxed, the man's muscled arms gave testimony to hard work and long hours. Every inch of him appeared sound and strong, aside from his broken leg.

They'd managed to transfer him to the cot in the surgery since hauling him upstairs to the spare bedroom was not an option. The cramped corner would have to do.

After Tay left to check on the Stanleys' new baby, Joseph Cooper's arm, and a half dozen other folks depending on his skill and generosity, Lena cleaned up the surgery and threw away the remains of their unconscious patient's shirt.

Oddly enough, his neckerchief remained intact. It hung sadly against his broad chest, and she worked the knot loose and dropped it on the trousers. Gray silk. Perhaps he was a cowboy rather than a sawyer.

With a cloth and a basin of warm water on the nearby washstand, she worked caked mud from the stranger's hair.

Except it wasn't all mud.

Bullet wounds had never made her squeamish unless she wasn't expecting them.

A neat, red line parted his hair just above his right ear—a wound understandably missed in Tay's examination of other injuries, considering their patient's bedraggled condition.

A breath closer, and the shot would have sliced off the top of his ear.

As if bathing a day-old infant, she gently washed the crease, then combed hair from either side of the crimson line. She washed his calloused hands as well, hardened and browned to match the lower half of his face. Gently, she pressed warm cloths against his angular chin and cheek bones, praying she didn't wake him.

In repose, his features were rather becoming, and she imaged his eyes blue as summer columbines, with lines that fanned from the corners when he smiled.

Scattering childish thoughts with a shake of her head, she added her apron to the soiled toweling, picked up the basin of dirty water, and paused for one final inspection. With his hair combed, his face clean, and his ruined clothing gone, he appeared fairly decent, though he still looked like he'd been dragged behind a team of horses and used to plow a field.

She dumped the water behind the house and set the basin in the kitchen sink where she half-filled it, then tipped in a portion of hot water from a steaming kettle. Tay was forever telling her that cleanliness was next to godliness, and she kept telling him it was closer to John Wesley than the Lord. But constant washing was now a habit she could not shake, and she rubbed the soap cake between her palms.

The morning's struggle with the stranger had taken everything she had and then some, but chores remained. With the back of her wrists, she pushed hair off her forehead, then took her bread bowl down. Minutes later, scooped flour mounded on the side board, a well dipped in the center awaiting yeast, sugar, and a little warm water.

She worked flour from the edges into the mix until it was soggy, pushed with the heel of her left hand, then added more flour. After hooking the satiny mound with a finger, she flipped it over and set to kneading.

Making bread didn't take much of a mind, and her thoughts migrated as they usually did during such chores.

Last Tay had told her, the Stanleys' baby was doing well in spite of coming a month early. He rode out every morning to check on the little thing. Mercy hadn't weighed more than a plucked chicken when she arrived, but young Mrs. Stanley seemed to be doing a fine job of caring for her firstborn.

Joseph Cooper was doing all right too after nearly cutting his arm off at the saw mill. Fool man got his shirt caught up in the workings. Another doctor might have amputated the mangled mess, thereby taking the man's livelihood as well.

Her left hand tingled, and she paused and twisted it in her apron until it was completely sheathed.

Tay wasn't like other doctors she'd known. He'd worked hard to save Mr. Cooper's arm, and he'd done it. By God's grace and gift, and a little help from her, he'd done it.

He'd worked hard for his title too. Buried himself in his studies that last winter at the cabin and every year after until he left for medical school.

In spite of his skill, townsfolk often joked behind his back about Doc Carver *carving* up his patients. If he minded, he didn't let it show.

She was proud of her brother, and often told him so. But something ate at him. She suspected what it was, yet he locked up like a steamer trunk every time she mentioned it. The same way he had when she was little and talked about the blue-eyed stranger. So she'd stopped mentioning him too.

Even Mama and Papa had sulled up like sour horses that winter and exchanged worried glances, as if she were daft or feather-headed. They never said so outright, but she could read the thoughts on their faces as plain as bobcat tracks in the snow.

Her hands rested on the board, and she gazed out the kitchen window. Sir Humphrey's grave marker jutted from the frozen ground near the old cabin, both of them weathered and gray. Papa hadn't torn down their first home when he built the big house. He and Mama had used the cabin for storage, and he kept the roof patched so rain and snow didn't ruin the inside.

Bitter and sweet warred every time she looked at it. On one hand, she was glad they'd kept the cabin because of what she'd seen there. Glad for the evidence that it wasn't all her imagination. Glad that Sir Humphrey rested nearby, for he'd been the only one to believe her.

Delirious was the word her parents whispered when they thought she was sleeping. She remembered that, but not the fever they claimed had caused it.

On the other hand—well, that was where the bitter came in.

A niggling sensation drew her attention over her shoulder and into the hallway. The stranger's even stranger dog lay across the surgery threshold, head on paws, watching her with hungry, mismatched eyes.

She pulled the bread dough into a round, plopped it in the bowl, and covered it with a towel. Then she plucked a hard biscuit from the chicken-scrap tin and broke it into a pie pan. A ladle-full of juice from the beans drizzled nicely over the dry pieces.

The dog made a whimpering noise.

She and Tay hadn't had a dog since Sir Humphrey, and she wasn't inclined to let this unusual animal eat inside.

Pan in hand, she went out the back door and walked around the side of the house, detouring purposely for a peek through the surgery window. She stepped soundlessly across her hibernating flower patch and peered through the slightly parted curtains, straight past the table to the doorway.

The dog was sitting up, staring at her.

She shivered.

Either she made as much noise as the neighbor's milk cow, or that creature was too crafty for comfort.

She continued around to the front porch, stomped off her high-top shoes, and opened the door.

"Come on," she coaxed, showing the pie pan at ground level and drawing it through the door. "Come out here and have something to eat."

The animal laid back down, ears sharp and skyward, eyes attentive with a vigilant not-on-your-life look.

"Suit yourself. I'll leave it out here on the porch. But you'd best be quick about it because the cats and critters around here will get it if you dally."

The dog turned its sleek silver head aside and blinked. If she didn't know better, she'd swear it understood every word she said.

Leaving the door ajar and the pan on the porch, she walked down the hallway to the kitchen where she filled an old chipped bowl with water. When she returned, the pie pan was empty. A quick turn toward the surgery doorway sloshed water on her skirt.

The dog blinked again and licked its jowls.

That evening at supper, Lena took the chair at the end of the table opposite Tay rather than her usual seat closer to the stove.

"What are you doing?" He paused, spoon halfway to his mouth, juice dripping into his bowl."

"Eating supper."

"Why are you sitting there all of a sudden?"

"Why does it matter?"

He took the bite and his head cocked the tiniest bit. A guarded movement, nearly imperceptible, but she'd been his sister long enough to catch the mannerism.

"You don't trust it, do you?"

Of course she didn't. "Of course I do."

A quick glance to her left confirmed her sense of being watched.

Tay chuckled, his mouth full.

She buttered a warm slice of bread, smoothing the pale, creamy yellow to the very edges of the crust, all the way around.

"You didn't say where you found him." The bread fairly melted in her mouth, validation of the county fair's blue ribbon in her top bureau drawer.

"With its owner."

She closed her eyes to keep from rolling them. "Not the dog, the man."

Tay spooned in another mouthful, took his time chewing, and finally swallowed. "With the dog."

So that was how it was going to be.

He laughed and threw his hand up, warding off her assault. "About halfway out to the Stanleys'. He was leaning against a tree, legs out straight and himself out cold. Looked like someone had propped him up there so I'd see him."

A shiver danced feather-light across her shoulders.

Against every table manner their mother had taught them, she dipped the corner of her bread into her beans and bit it off. Stalling. Waiting for Tay to continue his account.

"The dog was right next to him. Watched me like a coyote watches a gopher hole. I drove the buggy in as close as possible and sweet-talked my way past its curled lip."

He held both hands out across the table, turning them over back to front. "No bites."

At the other end of the hall, the dog still lay across the threshold, but its disarming eyes were closed.

"How'd you get him home?"

"With great difficulty. Dragged him up against a buggy wheel. Climbed in and pulled him across the floor boards, then drove home with my feet on the dash. The dog must have followed us. I didn't notice it again until I came back to the surgery with the extension board."

He shot her the same look their pa had when warning them not to argue. "Don't start on the table."

The words she'd already lined up rolled off her tongue one at a time and landed on a spoonful of beans she shouldn't be eating again. Wouldn't be eating again if people paid their bills in cash money rather than milk and side pork.

Then she remembered. "He was shot. Sort of."

Tay's spoon clattered to the bowl, and he shoved from the table.

Lena followed him down the hall, amazed that his racket did not wake their patient as well as every occupant of the town cemetery, including their parents.

"The right side of his head."

"Why didn't you tell me?"

She returned his glare on equal footing. "I just did. Would you rather I left him alone while I ran around the countryside looking for you?"

As Tay bent over the cot, his fingers probed along the salve-covered bullet crease. "No infection, it appears. No penetration. Just a graze."

He flicked a glance her way. "Nice work."

Haughtiness was always tempting but never worth the later repentance. "Thank you."

"We'll cast his leg in the morning. Swelling should be down by then. I'll sit with him tonight since you're scared of the dog."

The fine hair on her neck bristled. "I am not any more afraid of that dog than you are of courting Rebecca Owens."

Tay's brow reddened as if it were a summer day. He didn't argue with her. Couldn't argue with her, though she knew it wasn't fear that held him back, but rather, an unreasonable sense of brotherly responsibility where she was concerned. As if he owed her something.

The odd-eyed animal watched them both, appearing ready to pounce at its master's slightest grimace.

"I'll take the first turn," she said. "You need to be rested for your rounds."

The moon woke her to a chilled room, its full face shining through thin curtains at the window, stirring a memory. She tugged her shawl closer and arched her stiff back from the rocker. Its slight creak opened the dog's eyes. Just as watchful but less challenging, perhaps sensing she was friend, not foe.

She had, after all, given it food and water.

If only it could talk and tell her all that had happened to the tall, lean man who'd clearly been dragged. Not to mention nearly shot. His ravaged back and broken leg bore testimony to some of his story, but not to the cause of his injuries. Had he been thrown from his own horse, his foot caught in the stirrup as the animal charged away in a frenzy?

Had he been driving a wagon when mules broke from their harness and he, fighting to hang on to their reins, flew behind them over rock and ridge?

No. That wasn't it. He would have been face down if he were holding onto something. Something had been holding onto him.

She rose and stepped quietly to the cot. The dog lifted its eyes, watching her silent progress as she leaned low across the stranger to check his breathing—

His rough hand clamped her mouth, the other the back of her neck. Suspended inches from his dark, threatening glare, she couldn't move. Couldn't scream. Couldn't breathe.

Heart battering her chest, she clawed at his unrelenting fingers.

The dog stood, hot breath burning through her skirt with a throaty rumble.

Her compressed cry escaped on a prayer.

Still holding her, the stranger sat up and flinched. Sweat broke out on his forehead and caught the moon's light in pearly beads.

His grip weakened.

She pulled at his fingers and sucked in a breath only to waste it on a pointless promise. "I won't hurt you."

Something flickered in his shadowed stare and he glanced at the dog, its face nearly level with his own.

His hand pressed harder, cutting her nostrils with a soapy scent and the inside of her lip against a crooked tooth. The sound of her racing blood *whooshed* in her ears.

She forced a finger between his hand and her lips, but still her words were mangled. "We set your leg."

⁓

Wil Bergman flexed his left leg for balance. Pain knifed from his ankle to his brain, darkening his vision.

We? How many, and where were they now?

The woman filled his view, her pale hair fallen from its pins. She was no product of his nightmares. No wavering apparition. Fear burned in her wide eyes and pulsed beneath his fingers.

He could snap her fine bones like bird wings.

In a single sweep, he took in the small washstand, rocking chair, braided rug. A cabinet and long table in the shadows where moon and lamplight were thin.

The smell of antiseptic.

She continued digging at his fingers.

He squeezed. "Promise you won't scream."

She jerked her head down once. Less frantic than before.

"Where am I?" Slowly he released her.

A ravaged breath, and her chest heaved. Her hand clutched her throat. "In Dr. Taylor Carver's surgery— home."

"Where?"

"Piney Hill." Her gaze traveled the length of the blanket covering him, pausing at his bare feet. "Were you headed here for work at the saw mill?"

Awareness struck—his clothes were gone.

Something in her expression pressed him to tell her everything. "No."

She was calmer without his hands choking her. So was the dog, and it dropped to its haunches, close to the low cot, eyes shifting between him and the nurse. At least the woman seemed a nurse. That would explain her presence in the room at night and the full apron that covered her simple frock.

Where was the doctor?

She straightened, one hand lost in the wide apron, the other gripping the side of her skirt.

"I'll get another blanket for your feet."

He grabbed her left arm.

She resisted as though she held a hidden weapon—his reason for the sudden move.

The dog stood, bared its teeth.

With a vicious wrench, Wil twisted a cry from her throat and her hand from the white cloth.

She glared at him. Defiantly.

Whoa. He let go.

She moved slowly to a trunk behind the rocker, pulled out a wool blanket, then tented it over his lower legs.

It caved against his left foot, and even the slight pressure made him wince with pain.

Anger and compassion wrestled across her face. She took the lamp to the cabinet, where its dim light reflected off glass doors, then returned with a dark bottle and spoon.

The dog refused to move, so she reached over it with a spoonful. The smell banished all suspicion.

Wil preferred whiskey to laudanum, but doubted she'd provide it.

Her hand didn't tremble but held the spoon steadily in front of his mouth. Her regard was equally steady, and she raised one fine brow. "Well?" it asked.

If he wasn't in killing pain, he'd challenge that haughty question. Instead, he swallowed the offering and fell against the pillow, searing his back. Was there no place he didn't hurt?

With his left hand, he fingered a narrow piece of wood strapped to his leg, his greatest source of pain. A flash of memory closed his eyes—a gunshot. The ground racing past.

"What's your name?" The words clawed out of his throat.

"Lena," she whispered.

"Lena Carver?"

"Yes." She leaned slightly forward, the smell of cinnamon and nutmeg in her hair. "Can I get you anything?"

"Answers." Everything in him and about him hurt. Moving his mouth hurt. But aside from whiskey, he wanted answers the most. Answers to how he ended up in Dr. Taylor Carver's surgery with a self-appointed canine guardian. Answers for how Carver's wife managed to care for someone who had frightened her beyond forgiveness.

And answers for how she did what she did missing the last three fingers on her left hand.

CHAPTER 3

Lena jerked awake at the touch on her shoulder. Tay. The moon had fled, and in the flickering lamplight a shadowed groove danced between his brows. "What's wrong?"

"You startled me." She pushed her hair back and stood. The stranger lay as still as before, his chest rising and lowering, no sound of his breathing, no threatening moves.

Had she dreamed the encounter? A small cut inside her lip said no.

The dog watched Tay.

He picked up the laudanum bottle from the washstand. "Our patient came to?"

She fingered the tender place. "Yes. He was in a great deal of pain. Understandably so."

Tay studied her, possibly reading what she didn't want to tell.

"Did he hurt you?"

"No." The answer came reflexively, without intent to deceive. Without thought. She turned to trim the lamp. "How is someone with his injury going to hurt me? He has no gun, no knife, and no ability to rise from the cot."

"He still has one good leg."

"Which I could kick out from under him." She looked away, afraid the account of the man's iron grip would rush out on its own, without her consent.

"Did he say anything?"

"He asked where he was."

"What'd you tell him?"

"The truth."

His eyes narrowed. "What are you not telling me?"

The whole truth.

She pulled her shawl from the rocker and wrapped it around her shoulders on her way out of the room. "It's cold. I'll tend to the fire."

"Lena—"

Pausing at the door, she added, "The dog won't bother you. I'll bring coffee before sunup. He should be out for that long."

A few coals winked on the dining room hearth, and she stirred them before adding bits of kindling, larger sticks, and finally an arm-sized log. Smoke spiraled upward, then the smaller pieces caught and the fire flashed to life. She added two more logs, then set the screen in place and wound the mantle clock. Two-thirty.

The kitchen cook-stove fire had been well banked, and it took only a few cedar shavings to revive it and start a pot of coffee.

She twisted her hair into a knot and located three pins still clinging to tangles. They'd hold until she collected the others.

Too tired to work by lamplight and too tense to sleep, she returned to the dining room and pulled her rocker close to the hearth. The wind had kicked up, rattling Tay's sign on the front porch, swinging it noisily back and forth. They'd all need laudanum to sleep with that racket.

Through the cover of her shawl, she gently rubbed her tender wrist and wondered who had been more frightened—the stranger or her.

It was the uncovering that angered her. The brutal stripping away of her customary concealment.

The shock on his face betrayed what he thought. What everyone thought when they saw her deformity up close. The result of an uncertain doctor's attempt to save a little girl's hand.

She stared into the fire, seeing again the cabin hearth of her childhood, hearing her mother weep, Tay wretch. Papa held her in his big arms and pressed her head into his shoulder as the doctor eased her left arm from the safety of Papa's embrace…

As delayed as a child's anticipated Christmas, her hands began to tremble and she swaddled them in her shawl, annoyed at her lack of self-control. For twenty years she'd lived and managed. For the last five, she'd helped Tay, relinquishing dreams of her own home, a loving husband, children.

The older she grew, the more clearly she saw the way men averted their gazes. Polite, but uninterested. Who wanted a maimed wife? One who didn't even have the finger on which to place a wedding band?

Always, this time of year brought the heaviest torment. Always in the evenings approaching Christmas, when light fled and cold lurked around the house.

The smell of scorched coffee roused her, and she hurried to the kitchen and the boiling pot. How long had she huddled by the fire, lost in her musings? She ground more beans, added fresh water, and returned it to the stove.

Through the glass in the kitchen door, the sky was graying, melting the stars and waking the neighbors' rooster that seemed to relish rousing the community.

"*Er, er, er-roo,*" it cried.

In a moment an answer rang across the field. "*Er, er, er-roo.*"

Papa's voice shimmered through her memories, interpreting the early morning call from one proud bird to another.

Lock the barn door!
Give me the key!
Some things couldn't be forgotten.

~

The ceiling was white-washed.

Wil rubbed his eyes and blinked. White as milk and near blinding to a man accustomed to sky. He pushed up on his elbows and clenched his teeth at the impulse to yell. Moaning wasn't so easily squelched.

The dog raised its head over the cot's edge and studied him.

A light-haired man entered through the single door in the room and stopped short.

"Good morning." Grabbing a piano stool, he continued to the cot where he fixed the stool close by and sat upon it.

Wil looked around for the piano he must have missed the night before, but found none.

"How do you feel?" The man extended his hand. "I'm Dr. Carver, and you are…"

"In pain."

Humor livened the doctor's eyes, similar to his wife's, though clearly green. Maybe hers were too.

He maintained a professional demeanor and lowered his hand. "Indeed, you must be. My assistant and I have been trying to figure out what happened to you that would snap your fibula, dislocate your ankle, and flay your skin. We know what parted your hair."

Suddenly aware of the injury, Wil sat farther up and fingered the right side of his skull. Sure enough, a greasy line met his inspection and joined his growing list of painful spots.

The dog eyed Carver, at ease with his close proximity. Man must be who he said he was.

"How long have I been here?"

"Since yesterday morning." Carver turned up the wick, then lifted the lamp and leaned in. "Look straight over my shoulder and try not to blink. I want to check your eyes, see if you have a concussion."

"How'd I get here?"

Doc peered through his soul for a spell, then set the lamp on the table. Turned Wil's left wrist over and compared his pulse to the rhythm of an open-faced pocket watch. "I brought you."

While Carver followed the clock's hands, Wil took the man's measure. Not six feet, fine-boned but not frail. Again, similar to his wife.

Wil doubted the doctor could lift him. "Where'd you find me?"

Carver pocketed his watch. "What'd you say your name was again?"

Wil allowed the man had probably seen his share of broken limbs and gunshot wounds, and probably his share of liars, based on his narrowed green gaze. Since Wil's name was one of the few things he remembered, he might as well share it.

"Wil Bergman."

Recognition and curiosity collided in an ill-hidden stare.

Wil reached for his vest, clearly not hanging from his bare shoulders. "Where are my clothes?"

Doc collected himself and his professionalism. "Wasn't much left of them."

Wil's insides sank. "What about my coat and vest? And my hat." He sat up straighter and flinched, adding between clinched teeth, "My horse and tack."

Carver shook his head. "None of the above. Just you, one boot and sock, woolen trousers, a neckerchief—remarkably—and a shredded blue shirt, which we took the liberty of throwing away. Lena will have your trousers ready this afternoon, but I'm going to cast your leg first. The bones need to be immobilized, and this splint won't do it well enough. I'll find a nightshirt for you, since my shirts won't fit."

Stubbornness fired up through Wil's core, and he swung his legs over the edge of the cot. The wooden splint hit the floor, and pain shot him clean out of the saddle.

Carver grabbed him under the arms and helped him onto the infernal excuse for a bedroll. The ground would have served better, but not with a busted leg and no riggin'. No horse. And no idea what had happened.

He fell back onto the pillows, again thrashing tender skin, and bit down on a slew of cuss words that would paint that blasted ceiling blue and his ma red with shame.

Carver uncorked the brown bottle.

176

Wil shook his head. "I can't think as it is. No more of that poison. I prefer to dull the pain, not my mind. Do you have any whiskey?"

The doctor glanced over his shoulder, then set the laudanum on the washstand and went to the glass-doored cabinet across the room. Squatting before it, he opened a bottom door and reached his arm's length inside.

He returned with a tall unlabeled bottle and a short glass. "Kessler's best," he said, pouring half a glass. "But just between you and me."

Wil pushed up on his elbow, downed the liquid fire, and eased back again, waiting for the doctor to take a swig.

Instead, he corked the bottle and returned it to the cabinet.

At least Wil wasn't in the hands of a drunk. But he had no intention of ending up addicted to laudanum like too many sorry cusses he'd seen. He'd have to ride out the storm.

Hard to do without his horse.

Carver took his stool again, a whole battery of questions marching across his face.

Wil stalled him a second time. "Before you start, tell me exactly where you found me."

Doc braced a hand on each leg. "I was on my way out of town early yesterday morning, about to start my rounds, when I found you propped against a ponderosa pine about two miles north on the main road."

Wil must have telegraphed his doubt, because Carver chuckled and shook his head. "I know. Unbelievable. If I didn't know better, I'd say someone left you there so I'd find you."

He leaned slightly forward. "What's the last thing you remember?"

A movement at the doorway caught Wil's eye and interrupted Carver's inquisition.

"Lena, perfect timing." Doc rose and took a tray from her. "I'll hold this while you set the pillows up behind Mr. Bergman."

She paused, eyes shifting to the dog and then to the cot, avoiding Wil's. Sure enough, green like her husband's.

Closing in, she bent to arrange the pillows and clicked her tongue.

"Stay as you are, and I'll change your dressing. You've nearly rubbed everything off, including the salve. What have you two been doing? Arm wrestling?"

Doc set the tray on the long table and brought over two cups of coffee. The smell warmed Wil's senses and roused his stomach's hope for solid food in light of the whiskey in his belly.

An apology for brutalizing Mrs. Carver circled the back of his brain, but so did a wagonload of rocks.

She dressed his wounds, and after she finished, leaned toward his shoulder and sniffed.

He angled away. "I smell?"

She tucked the basin full of bloody bandages against her hip. "No, but Mr. Kessler does."

Doc coughed, bouncing his shoulders as well as coffee from the cups as he handed over Wil's.

The first sip went down hot, strong, and smooth, better than any trail coffee he'd had. "That hits the spot, Mrs. Carver. Thank you kindly."

She opened her mouth, but Doc spoke. "Lena is my sister."

The look she shot the doctor could have split a stump into kindling at a hundred yards.

CHAPTER 4

Wil had been sleeping on the cot for two weeks, and feared he'd go loco before long. Aside from Doc's help to the privy outside and the kitchen for meals, he was confined to the cramped corner or to the dining room they didn't use for dining. Where he sat now with his casted leg elevated on a chair near the hearth. A sight warmer than the surgery.

The dog lay in front of the hearth, halfway between him and Lena Carver, but watching him, not her.

Lena had ridden a wide circle around him until lately. A lively conversationalist at the table, she had an opinion about everything and didn't mind expressing it. Including her preference of *Lena* over *Miss Carver*. But otherwise, she managed to keep her distance from him, and Wil knew why.

His ma hadn't raised no heathen, and he felt like a heel for frightening the gal that night he came to with her in his face. But they were never alone for him to apologize. And he was fairly certain her brother didn't know what had happened. Letting him hear an apology might throw grease on an otherwise friendly fire.

All Wil could do was watch her in hopes of catching those green eyes, but she was a master at avoidance.

So was her brother when it came to talk of the livery.

If Wil had to drag himself into town, he would. Last he'd heard, his Uncle Otto owned the livery stable in Piney Hill, and Wil had written ahead that he was riding this way in hopes of wintering there, then scouting out the country. A gullet full of trail dust had put him in mind of his own herd and enough land that he could ride out a ways if the *settled* feeling got to be too much for him.

Colorado was as good a place as any to raise a few beeves, but his plans went slack somewhere between the road south from Denver and the outskirts of Piney Hill.

All those nights he'd stayed at camp when the boys lit out for the nearest bar to throw their money at liquor, cards, and women. All those months he'd added to his stash, rolling it in an old sock and tucking it deep in his saddlebags. All those dreams of having his own spread.

Everything he had was in his vest and saddlebags. Now his stake was gone, along with his good horse, saddle, and rifle. So was any memory of what happened to him. One day he'd accepted his pay, thanked the trail boss, and turned Duster south.

Next thing he knew, a beautiful woman was dangling from his hands, while railroad spikes drove through his busted leg with every heartbeat.

He owed the Carvers plenty. From what he'd seen delivered to the house and heard referenced at the supper table, Doc took anything for payment, from eggs and milk to bed sheets and horse feed.

But Wil didn't have anything to give the man and his sister. The shirt on his back belonged to someone else, some generous soul he didn't even know.

"How long before I'm sound enough to leave?"

Lena sat tearing bandages as if he didn't exist.

The doctor took off his spectacles, laid them on a medical book in his lap, and gave Wil a longsuffering look. The kind he might give a clueless child.

"You can't put full weight on it for another six weeks. The fibula needs time to reattach and heal solid. Without that happening, you'll be a cripple the rest of your life."

Same answer as the other two times he'd asked. Fewer weeks, but they still tallied up to eight.

And the answer still stuck in his craw.

He never had been good at confinement, the primary reason he'd left home as a kid and trailed that first herd. But wintering with his uncle had made sense. He could help. Curry and comb, muck stalls. Pitch hay and pay for his board. Nailing shoes on might be a stretch now, given his busted leg.

The timing couldn't be worse.

He leaned toward a stack of firewood at the end of the hearth, calculating how far he needed to go to get Lena's attention. A quick reach for a split log tipped the chair.

She looked up.

Using the log to brace himself, he locked on her, refusing to look away.

Beg your pardon, he mouthed.

Her eyes flicked to his lips and back. She puffed a sigh, then gave a short nod and went back to tearing strips.

Somewhat satisfied, he scooted to the edge of his chair and tossed the log onto the fire. "How far to the livery?"

Sister and brother exchanged a glance, and the spectacles came off again.

"Do you have a horse there?"

"Wish I knew. But I need to see if the owner is my uncle. If he is, he might have seen Duster or heard about what happened."

That stilled the bandage tearing.

"Duster?"

"My horse."

Doc fiddled with his eyeglasses, then smoothed his already smooth hair. "What'd you say your uncle's name was?"

As if he didn't know. "Otto Bergman. Big German, built like a tree."

Doc closed the book and laid it aside with the spectacles on top. "Think you could work crutches and *not* put weight on your leg?"

"I can crow hop, it that's what you're asking."

Lena's mouth curved in what some folks might consider a smile.

Her brother left the room, but she didn't follow him.

Wil leaned forward to scratch the top of his propped-up foot. "Is he always this talkative?"

The almost-smile flashed again, but she cut him a warning instead. "He's been holding off on the crutches because you're too eager to get on your feet. If you rush things, you could re-break your leg, get it infected, and slow your recovery. You need to just do what he says."

Her left hand slid under the apron.

He'd been staring and hadn't realized it. "I didn't mean to—"

"Stare?"

Her candor shamed him even further, but a *thud-clomp-thud* in the hall derailed his mental scrambling.

The bottom end of two crutches popped over the threshold, and the doctor swung himself through, landing on one foot. The other was bent up behind him. He crossed the room, turned, and crossed again before stopping in front of Wil and offering him two well-used wooden crutches, the tops wrapped in lamb's wool and doe skin.

"Let's see what you can do."

Wil took hold of the long, smooth brace pieces and slowly stood on his right leg. The crutches weren't long enough for his height, but at this point, he'd try branding irons.

One pass across the room was easier than he'd expected, but turning around was trickier. He felt like a newborn calf trying to gather its legs. Falling wasn't an option, and it near wore him out.

He pivoted and planted the wooden pegs, tempted to lower his left foot for balance.

"Don't do it." Carver had the same authoritative eyebrow Wil had seen on his sister.

He raised his foot, irritated by his weakened state and annoyed at how heavy the plaster was. "Can you take off the cast?"

"Absolutely not. Cross the room again. And don't set that left foot down or I'll tie it up."

Under different circumstances, he'd like to see Doc try it and not come away needing a cast himself.

He must have scowled, for Lena covered her mouth.

Two more passes across the room, and he had to sit down. More like fall down, but he did land in the chair.

"Not bad, not bad," Carver said as he picked up his spectacles and book. "Tomorrow morning, Lena can help you navigate the front steps, then you can take a spin around the house and cabin. I'll be making my calls, but if you're up to it after dinner, we'll go to the livery."

Lena's hornswoggled look boded poorly for her brother's recruiting tactics.

Wil didn't need an angry nursemaid telling him how to get around. He'd go to the livery on his own. "Where is it?"

"Farther than you think."

He didn't much cotton to the view from under somebody else's thumb. But he'd been out cold when he came to the Carvers' home and had no idea about the layout of the town. It couldn't be too different from every other wide spot in the road he'd ridden through, and he guessed the livery was at one end.

Or the other.

Hang fire. If touring the dining room winded him, he'd be a sorry sight if he chose the wrong end of town and had to hobble to the other.

Angry nursemaid it was.

~

The next morning, Lena pressed her mother's fluted biscuit cutter into soft dough and laid a dozen rounds in a baking pan. The day had just begun and already she was behind.

Honestly. Sometimes Tay was short-sighted as a blind turtle. Wasn't it bad enough that he'd pointed out her spinsterhood to a perfect stranger? Now she had to attend that stranger while he stumbled around on crutches that were too short. And with all she had to do.

Men!

With her wrist, she pushed hair out of her eyes, then topped the biscuits with a dash of cinnamon. Tay was, by nature, generous and caring, but not toward the blacksmith since the man had been so rude to her. It must be the Christmas spirit that prompted Tay's trip to the stables.

That same spirit was also prompting her. Six weeks was hardly time enough to keep up with all her regular chores, polish and clean the house for the big Christmas dinner, and finish the required baking.

Sliding the biscuit pan into the oven, she chided herself for using that costly cinnamon on breakfast rather than saving it for Christmas cookies.

Saving butter wasn't any easier, and they were down to their last mold. Davy Perkins had brought over fresh milk yesterday, which meant another chore today—churning. To go with baking and cleaning, and now touring the yard with Mr. Bergman.

Her thoughts stuttered at the name, considering the differences between uncle and nephew. Otto Bergman was the most unfriendly man she had ever met. He wanted nothing to do with neighborly charity or Christmas generosity, and warned her last year to stay away from his livery unless she had livestock-related business there.

Distance had been an easy thing to keep, a practice she'd also maintained with the nephew since she'd gotten too close on his first night in the surgery. Between his glass-eyed dog and his own lightning reflexes, she'd watched her step. But it was irritating, to say the least. This was her home. She shouldn't have to walk on eggshells.

All the more reason why his apology caught her off guard.

When she'd nodded her acceptance, the planes of his face softened in the fire's light, further surprising her. His expression appeared almost kind, in spite of his beard and family connections.

He'd nearly apologized again for staring at her hand, but Tay's arrival had prevented the pity she so despised. She saw it enough on everyone else's face. For some unprecedented reason, she did not want to see it on Wil Bergman's.

Never mind it. He'd soon be gone. Conversation would be more subdued at the kitchen table, and their daily routine would return to normal.

An unexpected note of sadness vibrated through her heart, like a single string plucked, its voice left to quiver and fade.

A telltale *clomp-thud* began at the other end of the house in muted accompaniment.

Wil's frustrated efforts at moving his angular frame on those short crutches last evening had been almost humorous. But he'd persevered, and for that he'd earned Tay's respect as well as hers.

She wiped her hands on her apron, then smoothed it over her skirt and tucked stray hairs into the knot at her neck.

And why shouldn't she respect him? She respected other men. Her father and brother. The pastor. Yes, Pastor Thornton. She respected him too. An honorable man who shared his faith in a clear manner without unnecessary adornment.

Respect for Wil Bergman was completely understandable. With perhaps a dash of pity for his predicament. But that was as far as it went. Absolutely no reason in the world to dread the day of his departure.

None at all.

She took a deep breath and smoothed her apron once more.

A final thump sounded directly behind her, snagging her breath.

"Mornin'." The smile in his voice lit her heart the same way the lamp brightened the pre-dawn kitchen.

"And good morning to you." She looked halfway over her shoulder. "Coffee's hot and breakfast won't be long."

Grateful for her busyness, she laid salt pork strips in a cold cast-iron skillet, then set it over the hottest part of the stove.

"How can I help?"

She glanced back. "Help?"

"Don't sound so surprised. I still have two good ha—"

Silence slid between them.

Her face tightened, her jaw clenched, and she whirled.

"Don't you dare. I am as I am—I have never known anything else. Figures of speech are a way of life, and I am comfortable with being different, so stop apologizing for something you have nothing to do with."

A burning began in her chest, worked up her neck, and into her face. She hadn't meant to lash out or be hurtful.

Hunching over on the crutches, he was nearly eye to eye with her. Dark, warm eyes that drew her, and she mustn't let them. She may enjoy his company—more than she cared to admit—but she didn't know this man. Didn't know where he'd come from, where he was going, or what he stood for.

But as he said, he *did* have two hands.

"Sit."

He frowned.

His dog obeyed, taking its place by the back door.

She pointed to the nearest chair at the kitchen table. "Right there. Sit down and I'll put you to work."

The butter churn invited her to scoot it from its corner with her foot while holding the dasher with one hand. Then she fetched the large jars of milk she'd left on the porch overnight to separate.

He looked like a child sent to cut a switch, and she couldn't contain her laughter. "Have you never churned butter, Mr. Bergman?"

His features hardened.

"Well, you offered, so this is your chore. Remove the churn's lid and pay attention."

"On one condition."

"I beg your pardon?" He had conditions? Of all the nerve. Perhaps her respect was misplaced after all.

He crossed his arms and set his shoulders. Even under the loose-fitting nightshirt, they presented a formidable defense.

She followed suit, and they held each other's gaze as if in a school-yard stare down.

His mouth hitched—what little she could see of it behind his untrimmed whiskers.

Breakfast would burn if she played this game any longer. "And what is your condition?"

"That you call me Wil."

His request dislodged her stoicism and she lowered her eyes, fearing that a blush would spread across her face.

He didn't play fair.

"Very well."

"Very well, what?"

The dreaded blush inched upward. A moment longer, and she'd be flashing hotter than the frying pork.

"Very well, *Wil*."

He smiled.

It was nearly her undoing.

She pulled a wooden ladle from her crock of cooking utensils and demonstrated how to carefully skim the cream into a bowl.

"From the bowl, pour the cream into the churn, return the lid, and start plunging."

He gave her a rather confidant look for a man who had never set his hand to such woman's work. But she had much to do and was fresh out of time for curiosity or sympathy.

Taking the crutches, she pulled out another chair and insisted he lift his leg to it. "You're all set."

Tay came downstairs and stopped at the kitchen door, clearly battling which role he should play—attending physician or teasing brother.

She poured coffee and set three cups on the table. Tay took his customary seat and gave her a mock scowl over the lip of his cup. "You'll have him so worn out, he won't be able to ride to town this afternoon."

The dasher hit hard against the bottom of the churn. "I'll be fine as flint and ready for it."

CHAPTER 5

Lena Carver, matched head to head with any trail-wise Cookie, and Wil'd put his money on her. If he had any.

As spirited a filly as he'd ever seen, she'd set him in his place twice that morning. And now she had him wearing a groove in fresh snow, riding herd around an old cabin not far from the house.

Four times he'd hobbled past a weathered marker that read *Sir Humphrey*.

This time, he jerked his chin at the gray board and fading letters. "Who's Sir Humphrey?"

She looked to the marker, her meadow eyes soft, cheeks pink with the cold. "Our dog. When Tay and I were growing up, Sir Humphrey was our playmate and guardian all rolled into one big hairy ball."

Her regard shifted back to the worn porch, straight peeled posts, and silvered logs of the cabin. Affection rested in her gaze.

"We lived in this cabin until I was about ten. Papa farmed. When the town grew out this way, he sold off some of the land. That money built the house and sent Tay to medical school."

The dog had trotted behind on Wil's first two circles. Now it sat on the narrow porch, watching as Wil stumped by. Blasted thing was laughing at him. He could see it in the glassy eye.

"Why didn't you get another dog?"

"Why don't you start a new path?" She shooed him away with her gloved hands. "You're down to mud and making a mess of things."

"This wasn't my idea, you know."

Exasperation puffed a white cloud from her rosy lips, and he worked himself over for thinking of Lena Carver in such colorful terms.

"Oh, all right," she conceded. "You can work on climbing the front steps."

He swung up onto the old porch next to his gray guardian. "How's that, General Carver?"

Hands at her hips, she shook her head, discounting his levity. "I think not, Mr. Bergman."

"We had a deal."

"What deal?"

"Lengthy labor for my given name."

Ignoring him, she headed for the house and slapped her skirt. "Come on. We'll show *Wil* how it's done."

Confounded dog up and followed her.

Leaving him behind, they marched along the path he'd flattened, then cut through a swath of unmarred snow, Lena's skirt lifted above her black boot tops.

He stopped halfway across. "You ever make angel pictures in the snow?"

She jarred to a standstill but didn't turn around.

"I can show you how."

The snow sparkled in the morning light, begging for someone to sweep three or four figures in the smooth, dry powder.

Lena hiked her skirt farther and ran around the front of the house, the dog close behind.

What had he said?

By the time he trudged to the porch, she was standing at the railing underneath a yellow-and-green sign hanging from two small chains: *Dr. Taylor Carver, M.D. & Surgeon.* Her arms were crossed high, both hands tucked under in opposition to the wide-open abandon required for flailing in the snow. Her face was just that white. Tight, and filled with pain.

"You all right?"

She nodded, but her lips rolled in and she wouldn't look at him.

He knew enough about womenfolk to know he didn't know enough. Nor did he have the right to pry into something she was hiding. Though he had to admit, he wanted to.

Three steps faced him, wide enough for two people to walk up side by side. He straightened, lifted the short crutches level with the bottom step, and followed with his right foot. The second step—*thud-clomp*—and the third, until he stood proudly on the porch. "Pretty good, don't you think?"

Another nod but not a word. She stared out across the snowy field at something only she could see.

After circling the cabin for an hour and then swinging himself across the field and up the front steps, he wouldn't have been able to fight his way out of a wet feed sack. But neither could he take her silence.

The sound of her voice had become what he wanted most to hear each morning. Sometimes he wondered how he'd lived nearly three decades without it.

Aching all the way from ankle to hip, he hopped to a rocker under the window, sank to it, and set his leg up on the porch swing.

If she got mad and gave him the boot, so be it. His question was worth a shot if it got her talking.

"I'm curious." No apologizing—she'd made that clear as white vinegar. "Since you grew up here, seems natural that you and your brother would have played in the snow." He would have if he'd not lived in more southern parts.

She didn't make a sound, just kept staring across the field in front of the cabin.

He leaned forward to pet the dog when a breathy answer floated to his ear.

"We did."

He'd nearly missed it.

"For a while, anyway. Until the Christmas I was four." Her whisper faded against the squawking of a jay off in the pines.

He strained to hear more.

"That's when I lost my fingers."

Something hard and heavy landed in his stomach. More than likely, his brain. He should have kept his fool mouth shut.

More questions crowded up against his teeth like cattle bunching for a storm, but he refused to let 'em run.

She dropped her hands and her shoulders slumped, and he had the crazy urge to get up and wrap his arms around her. Shield her from the memories and the struggle. Her defeated posture pained him since he'd been the cause.

Desperate to cheer her, he changed his tact. "Where'd you come up with a name like Sir Humphrey?"

With a deep sigh, like she was letting go of a weighty load, she rested her gloved hands on the rail. "Sounds rather regal, doesn't it?" She looked toward the cabin, giving him her profile. More regal than anything he'd seen between the Pecos and Wyoming.

"When he was a puppy, he'd curl up on the hearth with a *humph*. Sometimes he'd snort in his sleep. Papa thought it was a fitting name, considering the sounds he made."

She turned then, her expressive eyes latching onto his leg. "You must be hurting after all that traipsing around."

Her gaze met his briefly, then darted back to his cast. "I'll get you some tea."

As gently as he knew how, he reached for her right hand as she passed, expecting her to recoil from his touch.

She didn't.

"No laudanum."

She gave his hand a light squeeze before withdrawing her fingers. "No whiskey either."

In the short while she was gone, he tried to come up with all the ways he could have met Lena Carver other than the way he did. Every one of them involved blood or broken bones. Unless she went to church socials and such, which he hadn't had occasion to attend in some time.

Looked like pain was the only way he'd have found her.

A new habit of fingering the crease above his ear found his hair longer and in need of a trim. Further investigation along his jaw line confirmed that he was hairing up for a hard winter.

He hadn't let Cookie barber him like some of the boys did, so he was shaggy enough before he'd been ambushed. Being laid up here merely added to the problem. All the trouble with his leg had left him forgetful of how the rest of him appeared.

It was a wonder Lena Carver talked to him at all.

~

Lena stared into her cup, watching the level rise as she poured black tea, grateful she'd pulled herself out of shock over Wil's unexpected question about playing in the snow. The man was certainly full of surprises.

His simple query had stopped not only her feet, but her heart and her brain as well. She hadn't been able to think. Hadn't been able to catch her breath. It was a child's game he spoke of. Not one for a grown, mature woman.

Adults did not lie in the snow waving their arms and legs, but clearly, Wil Bergman did not know that.

She hadn't done it in twenty years.

Rousing her wits from such woolgathering, she returned to the porch with a tray and tea service and set it on a small table by the rocker. A teapot, two cups and saucers, sugar and cream, spoons, and a soup bone cluttered the surface.

Afraid to find his dark eyes bearing into her, she tossed the bone to his dog, who caught it in midair. No surprise there, for the dog watched her every move.

"Here you are." After offering Wil the empty cup and saucer, she poured in yellow tea. "Chamomile with a bit of willow bark. You should feel better soon."

He leaned forward, peering into her cup. "What are *you* drinking?"

"It's not Kessler's best, I can tell you that."

He snorted. "I'd have smelled it if it was." He cocked his head toward the dog. "Same way he smelled that soup bone."

The big dog propped the bone between both front paws as it gnawed, all the while watching Lena take a careful seat on the swing.

Wil lowered his foot to the porch, and she grabbed his trouser leg. "You'll do no such thing. We won't be here long, it'll get too cold. But if you want to wait out here for Tay, you'll be halfway to the livery when he gets back."

Puzzlement knit his brows until he followed her line of sight to the barn roof rising above a row of trees not a half mile from the house. Bold white letters painted across the dark wood were easily distinguishable: *Bergman's Livery*.

Clearly not amused, he scowled more deeply over his pale brew. "I thought your brother said it was a ways off."

"He said it was farther than you thought."

Sipping her tea, she studied him. "You seem the type to take off on your own if given half the chance."

If she wasn't on her toes, he'd hoodwink her again, like he had over the butter churn. He'd been anything but a novice and had probably helped his mother when he was a boy.

At the thought of toes, she considered his left foot, pointing skyward and propped beside her on the swing. She had worried that three wool socks were not enough to keep his foot from freezing. But he hadn't uttered a complaint. Getting out of the house was more than likely enough for someone like him. Someone who'd clearly spent most of his time outdoors, from the way he looked—and in a saddle, from the way he talked.

The best she could put together was that he'd been shot at, dragged, and robbed.

He remembered none of it.

"Did your brother set my leg by himself?" He tried his tea and grimaced.

"Of course not. Winnie helped."

That set him back. "Winnie?"

Teacup in hand, she was tempted to draw him into a ruse, but thought better of it. He could reach her with one of those crutches.

"Winnie is our buggy mare."

Better than a ruse. He choked on his chamomile and nearly spilled the entire cup.

For a man who had obviously traveled dustier trails than she, he was much too easy to tease. Choosing her words carefully, she explained their unconventional yet successful method of setting his bones end to end.

He studied her for a long minute. "You ride?"

Not a comment she had anticipated. "Why do you ask?"

"If you did, you'd make a hard-driving trail boss, is all I can say."

He smiled in a chuckling sort of way, and in spite of his grizzled beard and unshorn hair, she impulsively returned the gesture.

If she wasn't careful, she'd lose all of her composure.

Sleigh bells rang from behind a wooded patch, growing louder until Winnie herself trotted into view. Tay turned in next to the house, his breath rising in a cloud like the mare's. He jumped down, gloved and bundled, and ran his hand over Winnie's thick winter coat as he walked round.

At the bottom of the steps, he stomped off his boots, then joined Lena on the swing. The only man she knew who voluntarily attached sleigh bells to his buggy every November. Of course, he did it for her. She had loved their sound as a child.

Tay baited their guest. "You sure you want to do this?"

Suddenly Lena saw her brother's order of morning exercise for what it was—an effort to wear the patient down and send him to bed.

She stood and reached for the tray. "Dinner will be on the table in ten minutes. Plenty of time for you both to wash up."

CHAPTER 6

Wil tugged on the sleeves of his undersized borrowed coat, then grabbed his crutches. Doc Carver didn't seem any more eager for the short ride to town after dinner than he had before. More like he was trying to discourage someone from rolling through a cook fire.

He followed Carver down the steps and across to the buggy, figuring how he'd get up to the seat.

"Around back," Carver said, leading the way. "You can sit on the box. I'll take it slow so you don't bounce out."

He scraped mud off the edge of a shallow platform behind the buggy seat. It covered the rear axle and was nearly big enough to hold a picnic basket, but it'd have to do.

Back against it, Wil braced both hands on the edge and hopped up.

Carver handed him the wooden legs, dread pulling his face down like a shade on a window.

Sullen but good for his word, the doctor set the mare to a slow walk. Any slower and they'd be standin' still.

Wil felt like he was headed to the hoosegow.

It was the first time he'd approached anything in reverse, and it made him feel as if life was sneaking up on him. He couldn't see what was coming. People and store fronts just showed up. *Ambushed* was the word for it. Not a welcomed thought.

Piney Hill was pretty much as he'd imagined, except a lot smaller. A mercantile, bakery, and hardware store sprouted on one side, with a dry goods, bank, and jail on the other. He twisted around and saw the lumber mill tucked against the town's namesake off to the west.

The sweet smell of sawn wood drifted down but was soon overridden by the more familiar fragrance of hay and horse manure. Bergman's Livery was the last building on Main Street.

Carver pulled up parallel to the hitch rail and stopped with Wil right in front of the big double doors. The ping of hammer on steel rang from inside, and memories galloped out through the gaps between the barn boards. Wil was suddenly a kid again, watching his uncle shape red-hot steel on the anvil.

He paused before sliding off the box, waiting for the next inevitable sound, like the other shoe falling. Yet it wasn't a fall when it came, but the snake-like hiss of hot metal in water. He could almost smell the heat sizzling out on a rising ribbon of steam.

The mare bogged forward, jiggling the rig and reminding him why he was there. Easing down on his right leg, he plied the crutches. Doc Carson sat ramrod straight on the buggy seat.

"I won't be long."

His host and healer raised a hand signaling that he'd heard, but he didn't turn around, look back, or step down.

Completely out of character, based on what Wil had seen of the man, living in the same house with him and taking meals there.

But it wasn't any of his business. Finding his uncle was. He made for the doors.

The one on the right slid easily, and daylight wedged in ahead of him, thinning out toward the back of the livery. The hammering stopped. Wil stepped in and off to the side, waiting for his eyes to adjust before he headed down the alleyway.

Heavy footsteps approached, then stopped as Wil stumped into the light.

"Wilhelm?" The big man came closer, his expression doubtful. "Wilhelm, is it you?"

"Hello, Otto. Yeah, it's me."

"*Gott sei dank*!"

Next thing Wil knew, he was circled in a double-armed embrace that cinched him and his walking sticks as well.

Otto drew back and looked him up and down. "What happened to you, Wilhelm? I got your letter, but you never came." He tugged on Wil's arm. "Come and sit."

"I'm not stayin' today, but I wanted to follow up on my letter and tell you that I'll be back once I'm healed up, if you can use a hand."

A grin lit his uncle's broad face. "*Ja*. Is *gut*. I can use help from one I trust."

Otto's fire and a smoky lantern lit the back of the livery some and warmed things up enough that Wil wanted to take off his coat but didn't.

His uncle rolled a stump from against the wall. "Here. Sit. I have something to show you."

In a minute he returned carrying a saddle and saddle-bags.

Wil jumped to his feet, forgetting about the crutches until a sharp pain in his lower leg jabbed his memory.

"So it is yours." Otto hung the saddle on a low box-stall railing, the bags over the seat, then rubbed his finger across the underside of the cantle. "This brand is one I saw before."

A simple design Wil had burned into the leather when he left home. The brand he hoped would mark his own herd someday—Circle B.

He choked up for a minute, out of shock more than anything else, then lifted the near stirrup leather. Scarred, twisted, and stretched more than a little. His ankle twanged.

"Didn't happen to have chaps, a slicker, and bedroll tied on back did it?"

"*Nein.*"

"Where'd you find it?"

"On that fella out in the corral."

Christmas had come early.

Wil shoved the crutches under his arms and made for the back doors. Otto headed him off, lifted the bar, and swung them wide.

Daylight pinched Wil's eyes to a squint, but not so he couldn't make out a half dozen horses of varying color and size snoozing in the sunshine. A tail swished now and again, nothing too vigorous since the flies had all froze off and died.

He whistled low, and a dark head raised. Ears swiveled his way. A deep-chested rumble rolled across the corral, followed by a bay gelding that eased out of the bunch and sauntered up to him. Whiffled against his jacket, muzzle warm and familiar.

He gave one crutch to his uncle, then encircled the bay's neck, and ran his hand over its strong shoulders and down the front legs.

"You made it, Duster."

"He's sound," Otto said. "I checked him over good before I bought him."

"Bought off who?"

"A rangy pair in a hurry to sell."

Wil could name one or three fellas that fit that description and wouldn't mind gettin' his hands on 'em.

Otto approached the horse, stroked its side and hip. "All these years shoeing and tacking have taught me what to look for. When I saw your brand on the saddle but not you, I was afraid you'd been hurt or left for dead."

He came around the big bay and slapped a hand on Wil's shoulder. "It's good see you alive."

"I'll pay you back for him, I promise."

"With what, Wilhelm? The saddlebags were dark and empty as *stille nacht*."

Wil wasn't certain of that yet, but for the time being, he staved off disappointment. His war bag, slicker, and Winchester were gone, but he had his horse and his saddle. Things could be worse. In fact, they'd been worse about ten minutes ago.

"I'll work it off. After I heal up."

"*Ja.*" His uncle chuckled. "And how long until then?"

"After Christmas, Doc says."

Otto's face went cold. Put him in mind of Doc's when Wil told him his last name was Bergman.

"Carver?"

"He said he found me beside the road, propped against a ponderosa pine. He and his sister fixed me up with a cast and crutches. I've been stayin' at their place the last couple of weeks."

Otto went inside, taking the crutch with him.

Wil rubbed Duster behind the ears and earned a nuzzle. "I'll be back, boy."

Hobbling off, he realized he hadn't tried getting around on one crutch yet. It wouldn't have been so bad if the dang thing was longer.

At his anvil, Otto picked up a shoe that had grown cold on the horn and turned it in his big hands, reading it like other men read books.

Wil figured now was as good a time as any.

"What happened between you and the Carvers?"

Otto's black eyes shuttered like a school house in June.

"I will keep your Duster. Come when you can sleep in the office and be my night man." With a pair of long tongs, he pinched the horseshoe and shoved it in the fire.

End of conversation.

Again, Wil was left without answers. At least he had his horse, a welcome from the only family he had left, and a fairly good idea how he broke his leg.

It'd take a lifetime to earn back what he'd lost to the bushwhackers who ambushed him. A spread of his own now seemed as foolhardy a dream as ever.

He swung the saddlebags over his shoulder and headed for the big doors. It'd warmed up considerably outside.

~

As she had for several years, Lena found comfort in routine. The mundane. The doing of that which needed to be done. She pressed into such comfort again, rolling out pie crust for two pumpkin pies.

Wil Bergman ate as much as Winnie.

Though she had feigned reluctance at his conditional insistence, it had not been so hard to use his given name when addressing him, for she had begun to think of him in the intimate, informal way of close friends.

But the look on his face when he saw Bergman's Livery had nearly been her undoing. How would she feel if she were in a strange place, injured, and penniless? Family was family, regardless of how cantankerous some relations were.

The sleigh bells sounded above the slushy plod of horse hooves as the buggy passed the kitchen window, Tay alone in the seat.

Lena paused in pinching the pie crust edges. Had Wil stayed at the livery? Then her pulse quickened. Had there been an altercation?

Rubbing her floured hands against her apron, she hurried out the kitchen door as Tay reined in by the yard. Wil perched behind the buggy seat, splattered from head to three-socked toes with mud. Saddlebags hung over one shoulder, also splattered.

Relief drew laughter up from her insides, but she squelched it behind her hand.

Leaning dangerously low to set his crutches in the muddy drive, Wil dropped to his right foot and made his way to the back porch.

Still clamping her mouth, she lost the battle as he drew nearer, and an unladylike snort escaped.

He scowled up at her, looking as if he'd wallowed his way home rather than ridden. "That's a dangerous game you're playing there, Lena Carver."

His stern warning made her laugh harder, and she backed across the porch out of his reach.

"I'm so s-sor-ry," she choked.

"No, you are not."

"I'll set more water to boil so you can have a hot bath."

Halting on the bottom step, his scowl bore into her as if she'd been keeping an important secret from him. "You have a bath tub?"

"An entire bathing room. We're not as backwoods as you might think."

He looked around as if expecting to see it off by itself like the privy.

Understandable, she supposed. In his condition, he'd not seen the bathing room.

She opened a door and stepped aside for his inspection. "You have to come out here to get to it, but here it is, complete with hand pump. All that's needed is hot water, soap, and a towel."

He swung himself up the steps and across the porch, and took in the small room with its copper tub, her wash tub and ringer, and a hand pump. "You think Doc would let me use his razor?"

"I'm sure he would."

She gave him a quick once-over. "And you can borrow a pair of his britches, though they will be short."

The idea of those long, muscled legs in her brother's trousers was almost laughable. "We have another night shirt as well. I'll do up your clothes this evening and dry them in the kitchen overnight."

After such personal talk and private considerations, she could dry them by the warmth of her own skin, if what she felt was any indication. Turning, she left with an order. "Go on in. Tay will bring what you need."

Not waiting for his answer, she hurried through the kitchen door. Water was already warm in the stove's reservoir for washing supper dishes, but she added another pail full, then set a kettle to boil. By the time Tay saw to the mare and buggy, the water would be ready.

She slid the pies into the oven, checked the simmering soup, then hurried upstairs. Tay's razor and strap were where he always kept them at his washstand, and she found an extra pair of trousers in his chest of drawers. And more socks.

Downstairs, she chose a nightshirt from Tay's collection in the surgery, gathered a fresh towel and a soap cake, and piled everything on the table as Tay stomped up the back steps.

"These are for—your patient. He's in the bathing room waiting to wash away the other half of the road into town. Then come back for the kettle and a bucket of hot water."

Tay lifted his trousers. "Really?"

She waved him off. "They'll be short and narrow, but he can belt them on. We know the nightshirt will work."

Wil would also need help getting himself in the tub without submerging the cast, but she couldn't bring herself to mention it even to Tay. Surely he didn't need her to paint a picture.

CHAPTER 7

Helplessness was not in Wil's vocabulary, but as soon as Doc Carver told him not to get the cast wet, the idea of a good soaking hit like a maverick steer at the end of a short rope.

If he could get in the tub and hang his leg over the edge, everything would work out just fine.

But it was the gettin' in part that soured the deal, and he dang sure wasn't going to ask for help.

The best he could do was clean up while sittin' on a chair next to the tub.

He slicked his hair back, stropped the razor, and lathered his face. He'd shaved often enough on the trail that he didn't need a mirror. Still, it would have been convenient, but his own razor and glass were in his war bag, and Lord only knew where that was.

His saddlebags hung over the chair back, but first things first.

After as good a bath as possible, a stopper in the bottom invited him to pull it, and the water drained out. Beat bailin'.

Feeling more in control of things than he had since waking up in Carver's surgery, he rolled everything but the razor and strap into the towel and with a crutch, pushed it over near the wash tub. The idea of Lena washing his clothes made him twitchy, but she'd already done it once. Probably cleaned *him* up too, and he refused to think too hard on that. He'd been unconscious, so it shouldn't matter. Except it did.

He hadn't known her then—how her eyes lit up when that teasing streak took over, or how her voice rippled like music when she laughed. Too many times he'd caught himself day dreaming about what it'd be like to have someone like her on his place when he got one.

If he got one.

He lifted the saddlebags to his lap and unbuckled the near side. Reaching in, he ran his hand along the smooth bottom, feeling for a row of buck stitching along one edge.

Hope snagged on a tight knot at the end. This might be the best Christmas he'd had since he was a kid in Texas, but without his pocket knife, he'd have to wait to find out. He'd sewn the false leather bottom in tight enough to keep what coins he had from jingling. Apparently, it'd fooled the thieves.

An idea sprouted like spring grass, along with an image of Lena Carver walking through that grass. His grass. On his spread. He might be gettin' ahead of himself, but if his stake was secure, and he really did get the spread he'd saved for, then he'd have something to offer a wife.

Wife.

The word made him shiver and sweat at the same time.

He sat for a minute, pondering the notion. Looking at it straight on and admitting to himself that he'd taken the first step in that direction and done so without help of those blasted, short-legged hobbles.

The next step was figuring out if Lena felt the same. Two weeks wasn't long, but he'd spent every day of it with her. Hopefully, a couple more and he'd know if she'd have him.

He checked the other bag and found it like his Uncle Otto had said, dark and empty as a *stille nacht*. Interesting comparison, since that first *stille nacht* hadn't been exactly empty.

Slinging the bags over his shoulder, he picked up the strop and razor, suddenly caught by another idea. He sat down and reached into the near bag, pinched the knot between his thumb and forefinger, and applied the razor.

The November afternoon slapped Wil with a cold hand when he opened the door, and he prayed it wasn't a harbinger of Lena's reaction if he asked for her affections.

Ignoring that depressing thought, he focused instead on the dog coming at him, head low and sniffing.

"Just me, cleaned up some."

It looked almost relieved.

Low-bellied clouds bunched over mountains that bowled around the north end of the shallow valley where Piney Hill lay. The smell of snow hugged a growing breeze. Another storm comin' for sure.

Inside the warm kitchen, pumpkin pie was also comin' for sure. Wil hung his bags over a chair back.

Carver was washing up at the sink.

"Much obliged for the use of your razor."

Drying his hands, Carver turned and scrutinized Wil's face, no doubt looking for wounds to stitch up. "And a fine job you did."

At supper, Wil caught Lena watching him as if he were a stranger. He should have checked himself in the mirror by the hall tree before he sat down. But the sweet aroma of a home-cooked meal won out and he stayed put.

A bowl of stew and a quarter pie later, Carver laid his fork on his plate and leaned back in his chair, satisfied as a milk-fed pup.

"You out-did yourself tonight, Lena."

Wil agreed. "Thank you for supper, Miss Lena. And for the extra clothes, Doc."

Carver chuckled. "They'll do until tomorrow." A sparkle lit his eye. "Thanks for cleaning up so well."

Wil expected a comment like that from Lena, not her sober brother. Especially after the solemn ride to the livery.

He shoved his hair back. "Soon as I'm out of this plaster, I'll get in to the barber and clean up even better. You won't know me."

"No need. Lena can cut it for you. She cuts mine."

Doc Carver was sure one for volunteering his sister's services without her say so.

She sat lock-jawed in her place at the table, staring a hole clean through her sibling.

Wil wasn't sure he could handle her running her fingers through his hair right now, but he wouldn't mind finding out.

A rosy tint ran up her pretty neck and into her cheeks, and she shifted her eyes to the remains of her pie.

Doc took his plate and bowl to the dishpan. "Isn't that right, Lee?"

Lee?

If looks could ground-tie a man, Doc'd be spending the night in the kitchen. As it was, he shrugged into an old coat and gloves. "I'll be chopping kindling."

He left, tugging the door hard against a gusty wind.

Silence fell harder. No smiles. No light-hearted banter.

Wil cleared his throat. "Thanks again for supper. Especially the pie."

He might as well take up public speaking, seeing he had such a gift for oratory.

The dog groaned from its place by the door, the traitor.

Lena stood and whisked his dishes away. "Stay where you are, and I'll see what I can do with your hair. Otherwise you might not find your way to the cot."

Once her feet hit the stairway, he grabbed a crutch with one hand and the pie pan with the other, then managed to clear the rest of the table and shave soap into the dish pan before she returned.

Pausing at the doorway, she took in what little he'd accomplished, and a pleased expression set in place.

"Since you're over there, grab a tea towel from the second drawer." She pulled a chair from the table.

He straightened to his full height and held the crutch with his left hand. "You're not puttin' a bowl on my head."

Her mouth quirked and her eyes snapped. "I wouldn't think of it." She indicated the chair. "Now, if you'll please take a seat, I'll lower your ears."

Relieved—a little—by her joviality, he complied.

She took the towel from him and draped it over his shoulders. Then lifting the fringes of his hair, she tucked the towel inside the nightshirt, all the way around his neck.

Her warm hands grazed his skin in the process, and for all he was worth, he couldn't recall a barber ever increasing his blood pressure like she did. Maybe this wasn't such a good idea.

But when she came around in front of him and pushed her fingers through his hair, her skirt brushed his knees and the smell of her brushed his good sense, and he prayed his manners would survive the coming ordeal.

~

Smoothing the towel in place, Lena ran her right hand over Wil's shoulder, exactly like she did Tay. But Wil Bergman tensed up, rigid as a barn door. Did he find her repulsive? Did he doubt she could do the job, given her *condition*?

Never mind it. Tucking her chin, she pulled in a deep breath, drew a comb and scissors from her apron pocket, and circled behind him. She'd not be put off by his doubts when she knew she was perfectly capable of the chore, despite how many fingers she did or did not have.

Guiding the comb through his long hair, from his forehead straight back, she repeated the move, careful not to gouge the bullet trail above his ear. As she combed in easy, repetitive movements, his shoulders relaxed. Tension lifted like steam off fresh bread from the oven.

He sighed and sank against the chair.

When she stepped to her right, she could see his eyes were closed.

A bit disconcerting. Tay had never reacted this way when she cut his hair. Theirs was usually a lively, teasing banter, with her threatening to nick his ears.

But Tay was her brother. And he didn't have a mass of hair that flowed through her fingers like dark silk. Nor were his shoulders so broad and straight. Wil Bergman filled the chair, the entire room, for that matter, and his scent swept around her. Clean. Strong. Masculine.

She'd best keep her mind on the task, or she'd be sighing as well.

Switching the comb to her left hand, she held it between thumb and forefinger, lifting sections of hair and cutting along the comb's edge. Then she worked around in front of him, combing his hair back again, distracted momentarily by movement beneath his eyelids. What was he thinking? What was he feeling? What would it be like to—

Snip.

Oh dear. She combed up the same section, evening out what she had done, praying he didn't notice when he viewed the results of her barbering skills.

Clippings fell from her scissors to the towel and the floor. She trimmed her way around him, stepping over his extended leg, and shortening his hair to just above his collar. After finishing, she studied the overall affect.

The line of his jaw was clearly visible since he'd shaved, his mouth firm yet kind. His brows still cut a sharp contrast to his pale forehead, but he looked nothing like the wild-eyed man who'd held her in a death grip that first night in the surgery.

Then he opened his eyes.

Dark and deep, they locked onto her, holding her as firmly as he had before. Something in his gaze drew her, *begged* her, matched a longing in her heart note for note, and she could not move or look away.

A gusty blow slammed the kitchen door opened, and Tay tromped in with an armload of wood for the cook stove.

Lena filled her lungs with cold air—the first breath in how many moments?

Wil Bergman's mouth tipped on one side. No mockery. No sneer. More like something akin to pleasure. Something she'd never seen on a man's face.

"Well?" he said.

She blinked. Watched his mouth widen in a full smile.

"How do I look?"

"Oh. You look fine." *More than fine.* She dropped the comb and scissors into her apron pocket and folded her arms, reaching desperately for detached composure.

"Almost civilized," Tay blurted as he shut the door. "There's a mirror at the other end of the hall."

Wil grabbed a crutch.

"Wait." She combed through his hair for stray clippings, then removed the towel and folded it into a bundle for shaking outside. She'd wash it tonight with his mud-spattered clothes—a concession she'd not make for herself or Tay.

After Wil left, she laid the bundle on the table and fetched the broom and dustpan from the pantry, counting off the reasons why she shouldn't beat Tay with it and sweep him outdoors for getting her into this fix.

She came up with only one.

Two, when she found him leaning against the counter eating pie with his fingers, beaming mischievously as if he were twelve.

"I knew you could do it."

"Don't talk with your mouth full."

He snorted, then choked on the last bite. Served him right.

She swept the floor clean and gathered the bundle.

"No harm done, Lee."

Maybe not to you. "You had no right."

Tay came close and laid a hand on her arm. "He's a good man, Lee. I feel it in my bones. You get to know a person living with them day in and day out. I think you know it too. You're different with him here. You've laughed more in the last few weeks than in the last year."

She pulled back, kept her jaw clenched. If she opened her mouth, all her hopes and dreams might come spilling out. And for what purpose? To what end?

The last question broke her resolve.

"No man wants deformity, Tay. Hasn't that been clear enough over the years? Besides, the only thing we really know about him is he's a Bergman. He's probably just like his uncle, but we haven't seen it yet."

Tears marshalled at the accusation she knew was unfair and unproven. "Bring the kettle out to me when it boils."

Tay started to speak, but she opened the door to a brutal wind. It whipped around the house and across the porch, stinging her eyes.

She made it to the wash room before the tears fell.

CHAPTER 8

Morning poked its head through the window, a sleepy one-eyed approach. Daylight came so late these days, it felt like near noon before it got around to showing up.

Wil scrubbed his hands over the top of his head and stared at the white-washed ceiling. He'd almost forgotten how it felt to be shorn and sheared. It'd taken a while to get used to the new look, and he checked the hall mirror every time he hobbled by, makin' sure he was still the same person.

He checked his saddlebags too. Not that Doc Carver and his sister would steal his stash, but seeing the lumpy sock had a way of easing his worry where Lena was concerned.

She'd done more than help set his leg, feed him back to health, and cut his hair—something he'd *never* forget.

She'd burrowed under his saddle blanket.

Likely, she didn't know it.

He needed to tell her. But not until he had a new suit of clothes, *two* boots, and some idea of what he was going to give her for Christmas.

He threw off the quilt and sat up, confident of what he'd give Doc. He was going to pay his bill in real cash money. But he didn't have a clue what to give Lena.

Other than his ma, he'd never given a woman anything but a hard time. After pulling on his clothes, he reached for a crutch. One suited him now.

Talk at the supper table lately had been about gettin' ready for Christmas Eve at the church and the big feed here the next day. He was halfway to his eight-week mark and itching to get shuck of his cast in more ways than one. He'd gone to running a thin branch down inside the plaster to scratch what itched.

Trouble was, that twig didn't do him a lick of good when it came to Lena Carver. She was an itch he couldn't reach. Four weeks and he'd be bunking at the livery, missing her quick wit and smile. Her good cooking. The music of her laughter.

It was harder and harder to be around her and not spill his oats right there in front of her, Doc, and the good Lord all at the same time.

As he neared the kitchen, the smell of gingerbread drew him back to childhood and the warmth of his ma's quick hug after she gave him a couple of ginger cookies. One for each hand, she always said.

He stopped outside the doorway to the kitchen, listening to Lena busy at the stove. Walking back and forth to the table, pausing at the sink, checking the oven, stirring gravy. The smells swirled together, tugging at his stomach as well as his memory.

Was he crazy to think she might consider being a rancher's wife? After he bought a spread and a small herd, would she up and leave town and her brother's practice for life with a cowboy, bawling cattle, and fluctuating beef prices?

What if he couldn't build her a house this nice, with a parlor, an upstairs, and an entire room devoted to washing bodies and clothes?

His prospects were looking bleaker by the minute.

"Are you coming in here, or are you going to stand in the hallway all morning?"

Shock gave way to concern when a crash sent him loping into the kitchen. Lena stood over a tray of ginger cookies scattered on the floor in front of the stove.

One long swing landed him next to her, holding the crutch for balance and bending in half to grab the pan. "You all right?"

"Here." She shoved a towel at him. "That pan is hot as the dickens."

Feelin' handy as a hog at a picnic, he managed to set the pan and towel on the stovetop. "Why, Miss Carver. Such language."

With his left leg out straight, he stooped to grab a half dozen cookies off the floor, then returned them to the pan.

She snatched the towel and flicked it at him. "Don't you *Miss Carver* me."

He caught the towel and pulled her closer. "Which hand did you burn?"

Her cheeks pinked like a summer rose.

Leaning on his crutch, he took hold of her wrists. She pulled back, but he held on, gentle-like, until she looked him in the eye.

"Did you forget to use a hot pad?"

She made that little huffing sound of hers and glanced away, but he tugged again. He wanted to see inside her, read what she was thinking.

Finally she gave in and her arms relaxed. Her head tipped to the side like she was humoring him.

"You heard my ol' peg leg in the hall, didn't you?"

"Yes. It is rather hard to miss, you know."

"And you got distracted when I didn't show up."

Her cheeks flamed darker.

"Am I right?"

He was pushing his luck and he knew it, but four weeks was four weeks, and he didn't get opportunities like this every day.

She'd fisted both hands and held them down so he couldn't see her fingers.

He turned them over. The left one was redder than the right.

He was close enough to the sink to pump cold water onto a clean rag from the counter, and he did so without letting go of her arm. Then he squeezed it out and pressed it against her palm. After closing her finger and thumb over it, he turned her hand over and raised it slowly to his lips.

Her breath caught, but she didn't pull away.

Hunched on his crutch like he was, he had a clear view straight into her meadow-green gaze.

Her eyes fluttered shut and her lips trembled. He wanted to kiss them too, but if she shoved him, he'd end up on his southern side, and that wasn't the impression he wanted to make.

He held her hand until her eyes opened, shining like a spring puddle after rain. Words deserted him. Giving a quick squeeze, he let go and stepped back.

She didn't speak, but she didn't shy away either. Just stood looking down at the apron she'd bunched.

Hope lurched.

The dog scratched at the door, shattering the moment. Fool animal had pitiful timing.

Lena snickered and gave him two broken cookies off the tray.

He smiled. "One for each hand?"

"No. One for the dog."

At least she hadn't chewed him out for taking liberties. But he'd meant no disrespect. Just the opposite.

He followed the dog out, missing Lena something fierce, and he wasn't even gone yet. Pulling in a cold draught, he took in the sky, clear as glass. The sun bright, sparkling on the fresh white blanket that lay smooth across the fields.

Perfect for making snow figures.

Fool notion for a man his age, but for some reason he couldn't shake it.

~

Lena had never been so eager for Tay to leave as she was today, for he took Wil with him, not on rounds, but to town for clothes.

After this morning's unsettling affair with the ruined batch of gingerbread men, she could hardly think straight.

Wil Bergman had done quite more than recover the dropped cookie sheet and kiss her scarred hand.

He'd completely disarmed her.

She hadn't picked up her coffee cup once during breakfast for fear that she'd tremble the contents all over her plate and the tablecloth, not to mention her lap.

After they left, she tried desperately to fit Wil's actions into a logical explanation. But his tender strength and the gentleness of his lips on her hand left her light-headed and yearning again for things set aside long ago.

Ever since he'd come back from his uncle's with those saddlebags, he'd been livelier. He carried a sense of purpose, as if hope had lit a hidden wick inside him.

He'd talked about his reason for coming to Piney Hill. His resurrected plans to buy a "spread," as he called it, and populate it with cattle. As happy as she was for him, she was not happy for herself because he'd soon be leaving them and moving into the livery with his uncle.

Another loss at Christmas.

She pushed that thought away. Her selfishness shamed her.

Again, she took refuge in the mundane. Sweeping, dusting, tidying. Keeping the fires going in the dining room and kitchen and her thoughts on doing rather than feeling. She set beans to simmer and baked another test batch of cookies, though she could mix them up and lay them out in her sleep, she'd done it so often.

With everything finished that she could think of, she ran upstairs for her knitting.

The old bitter-sweet tug of the season leveraged against her like a see-saw, pulling her up and then dropping her low.

But the lows had been fewer with Wil Bergman around.

Reaching beneath her bed, she pulled her knitting basket from its hiding place. Not that Tay would come looking, but trying to keep his gift a surprise was nearly impossible. Hopefully she'd have an hour or so to work on his wool cap and scarf while he and Wil were gone.

Downstairs, she drew her rocker close to the hearth and inventoried her yarn, pleased to find enough brown to make a scarf for Wil. The lovely warm color matched his dark hair.

Perhaps he would think of her on cold blustery days at his ranch.

Shaking off her melancholy once more, she took up Tay's sage green cap, a fitting complement for his eyes.

Giving was her antidote against the crushing sense of loss that attended each Christmas. Giving and deliberate gratitude. It kept her mind from despair when she counted off her blessings—a kind and competent brother, a warm home, and food enough. A few friends at the small church, and children there to make up for those she would never have.

So each year, she threw herself into the festivities, as simple as they were. And the meal she and Tay shared with all who would come on Christmas Day. Each contributed something—a pie, preserves, sweet potatoes, starched linens, cider. She invited everyone she knew and a few she did not. Former patients, neighbors. The smithy.

Her neck and shoulders tightened. Such an invitation had begun the rift between them somehow. She still did not understand his harsh reaction, as if he hated Christmas and everything it stood for.

But in spite of Otto Bergman and his cold shoulder, life was not so bad. She could have lost the whole of it those twenty years ago rather than a few fingers.

Comfort slid around her like loving arms— providential provision, she knew. *When I sit in darkness, the Lord shall be a light unto me.* Hadn't Pastor Thornton mentioned that verse just last Sunday?

As her needles softly clicked, creating one stitch and then another, she thanked the Lord again for her odd approach to what other women took for granted. They might scoff at her unorthodox method, holding the left needle with thumb and forefinger and propping it against her stomach, working the yarn with her right hand. But she had produced many a cap over the years. Mittens, shawls, and socks too.

It warmed her to think that her labor would in turn keep warm the men for whom she cared the most.

~

Already the road to town was melting into muck, and Piney Hill's Main Street looked like someone had poured a river of hot cocoa between the buildings.

But Wil had a new idea. Two, in fact, and both required a stop at the livery.

Doc stayed in the buggy again.

"*Hallo, Wilhelm.*" Otto met him halfway up the alleyway between stalls, gripping his hand like the smithy he was. "You are still in the cast."

"And will be until after Christmas. But I need a couple of favors."

"*Ja?*"

"First, a stump out by your hitch rail so I can climb up to the buggy seat when we leave. I'm not ridin' on the back again in this soup."

Otto peered out the door. "I can do this."

"Next, I need to use your nippers. And a large empty tin, if you have one."

Otto raised his chin and peered down his nose at Wil as if he'd lost his bearings.

"I'm making something for Miss Lena."

At that, the big man *whuffled* like an old horse, but he went to his office and came back with a peach tin still sticky with juice.

"*Danke*," Wil said, the old word spilling out without any forethought. "I'll be back shortly to work on this."

If Otto had hard feelings against the Carvers, particularly Lena, things might get ugly. Pa had always said blood was thicker than water, but as far as Wil could figure, Lena had cleaned up more of his blood than his uncle ever had.

He still owed the man, and he'd be sure to show respect. But he might have to find work elsewhere.

Wil trudged through the melting snow between the livery and the hitch rail and stopped next to Doc. "I'll be gettin' some clothes and meet you here in an hour."

Surprise straightened Doc's back, and he gave Wil a thorough once- or twice-over. "You could fall in this muck, with only one crutch."

"And I could do just fine."

Doc didn't have much say in the matter since he couldn't pick Wil up and plant him on the buggy box.

"Otto's gettin' me a step so I can climb up to the seat for the return trip. I'm not showin' up at the house again all mud-splattered from ridin' on that buggy box."

Doc's features cinched tight, but he conceded. Again, no choice.

He looked over his shoulder and pointed with his chin. "Two blocks back on this side. Owens' Dry Goods. If they don't have what you need, check at the mercantile across the street."

Wil raised his hand to a hat brim that wasn't there. Another item for his list.

"Is there a land office in town?"

Winnie stepped forward, out of sheer boredom, Wil figured.

Doc pulled her in. "Next block past Owens'."

The sun told Wil he had more than two hours till noon. He needed only one. "What time is it?"

Doc checked his pocket watch. "Half past nine."

"I'll see you in an hour."

Doc was right about more than the time. It was tough goin' in the mud before Wil reached the boardwalk. Slick as snot through a tin horn. And he was sure he knew the origin of that old saw "stick in the mud."

Owens' Dry Goods had what he needed—trousers, two shirts, under riggin's, and boots that would do for now. A stockman's knife and a good John B. wide-brim, high-crown Stetson that set him back eight dollars. Razor and brush, and a blanket-lined canvas coat. He didn't have immediate need for a rifle and slicker, so they could wait.

Owens' daughter made sure Wil knew who she was as she wrapped his purchases in brown paper and string, mentioning Doc Carver's name a half dozen times in the process. Wil could read sign. Didn't take a genius to see who she'd set her cap for.

Good storekeep that she was, she didn't even twitch when he pulled his old rolled-up sock from his boot top and paid with a Double Eagle.

He slapped on his new hat and headed for the land office, where news wasn't as encouraging. Not as many sections for sale as he'd hoped. But a couple were worth checking out as soon as he could ride. Course, by then it'd be the dead of winter.

However, one thing Wil had going for him was worth more than all the money in his sock and all the land in Colorado.

Hope.

He hadn't survived this whole mess to give up now. Plus he had a little more motivation than he did a month ago.

Doc was waiting when Wil made it back to the livery. So was a stump standing next to the hitch rail's near post.

Wil handed up his parcels. "I've got one more thing to do. Can you wait?"

"Sure." Doc cut a side glance toward the livery's big double doors like he didn't think too highly of the proprietor.

"I won't be long."

And he wasn't. It didn't take but a minute to cut the tin into three rounds, slice out the bottom, and file the edges smooth.

Otto watched him with sullen interest but said not a word.

When he finished, Wil tipped his hat. It felt good. "Obliged."

Otto nodded and stoked his fire.

Wil turned for the alleyway, then stopped. "You goin' to Christmas Eve at the church?"

Otto snorted louder than his billows. A dark glare Wil's way was answer enough.

His guess must be right, but even so, his uncle had no cause to take it out on the Carvers.

At the buggy, he passed the tin pieces to Doc, then leaning on the crutch, stepped up on the stump. The buggy was close enough for Wil to plant the crutch, grab hold of the seat's arm rail, and swing in.

"Miss Owens said to tell you howdy."

Doc didn't look at him, just shook the reins and got red in the face. Winnie sucked her hooves out of the mud and plodded ahead. Apparently, the mare didn't enjoy the effort any more than Wil had.

As they approached the road that turned off toward the Carvers' place, Wil threw the fat in the fire.

"If you don't mind my asking, Doc, how did you and Otto get cross-ways?"

CHAPTER 9

Wil dropped the tin pieces in his hat and set it lightly on. With Doc's help, he got all his parcels out of the buggy and past the dining room door without Lena asking any questions.

After Doc left to tend to the buggy, Wil shoved a few things under his cot and pulled the blankets back. He unfolded and spread out his new clothes, then covered them with the blankets. No self-respecting cowboy wore creased britches, lookin' like he'd just pulled 'em off a store shelf. Though he had.

With a winded heave, he collapsed on the cot. He'd done more in one morning than he had in a month, and his body didn't mind telling his brain it wasn't happy with him.

The dog trotted in and dropped down next to the cot with a similar grunt.

Not long after, quick footsteps on the staircase took Lena to her room and back down again. No footsteps at all meant she was tiptoeing to the surgery to check on him. For nursing or for other reasons, he wasn't sure, but he'd take either.

The movement of her skirt gave her away, plus a whiff of cinnamon that had forever imprinted her in his mind. She stopped by his feet, her voice soft.

"Are you in pain? Or hungry?"

He couldn't help himself. A smile broke out like measles, and he opened one eye. "Not much and always."

She tipped her head in that way she had, tilting his heart with it. He pushed up on his elbows. Prettiest gal he'd ever known, but he didn't think *she* knew it. How to tell her without runnin' her off?

"I have some hot soup on the stove. Coffee too."

"Cookies?"

That brought her hands to her hips and a snap to her eyes.

"You didn't feed 'em all to the dog while I was gone, did you?"

It raised its head, and she glanced at it. "Now, there's an idea."

She whirled and her dark skirt fanned out, and he had a sudden vision of dancing across the room with her.

With his cast and crutch, there'd be no dancing anytime soon, and he laid back and tried not to think about it.

He must have dozed off, for at a strange sound, he came upright, braced for battle. She was setting a tray on the table next to him. Soup and coffee sloshed.

Her eyes were wide and dark as pine trees, not meadow soft. He'd frightened her again.

"Beg pardon, Lena. Don't know why I'm jumpy as a jackrabbit."

Using the folded napkin, she sopped the spill. "Maybe it has something to do with your injury." She looked him up and down as if huntin' clues. "Do you remember anything about what happened?"

"Wish I did. But after seein' my saddle and stirrup at the livery, I think Duster must have dragged me a ways."

She picked up the tray and transferred it to his lap. "Tay and I thought the same thing. When he brought you in, you looked like someone had plowed a field with you."

"Felt like it too." He spooned in the soup, eyeing a couple of cookie pieces on the backside of the teacup saucer.

"My ma made gingerbread men at Christmas. Just like these."

"Broken?"

Tickled, he sputtered against his spoon.

"I'll get you another napkin."

"No." He reached for her arm, then drew back. "I mean—stay. If you don't mind."

She blinked and fussed with her apron.

"You could sit with me while I eat."

Avoiding his eyes, she slipped something from her apron pocket to the dog, then pulled the rocker closer and sat down, hiding her hands in her apron.

Steaming coffee, thick soup, and beautiful company. Maybe he'd died and made it to heaven after all.

She let him eat in silence, her hands fidgeting under the white fabric like they needed something to do. She didn't jabber like some folks, and he imagined she could sit out by a campfire at night and enjoy the quiet as much as he did. He imagined—

"Did you get everything you needed in town?"

He laid his spoon aside and dunked a cookie in his coffee. "Not everything. But I will in time."

She watched the broken ginger man travel from his coffee cup to his mouth.

"I suppose dunkin' cookies isn't proper here."

Her laugh fluttered out, soft-like. "Oh, it's not improper at our table. Maybe at the Christmas Eve party at church…"

She stalled and looked straight at him. "You are coming, aren't you?"

Wild horses and real plows couldn't keep him from it. "If you'll have me."

Bad choice of words.

"I mean, if it's open to the public, yes, ma'am. I should be walkin' on two legs by then."

Her easy smile made him warm on the inside, and he couldn't figure how he'd live after Christmas if she wasn't with him.

"I'd best get to work." She stood and picked up the tray.

He kept the coffee and raised the final cookie. "Do you make other shapes besides busted-up men?"

"Very funny." She balanced the tray on her hip. "Stars and trees. Circles. Simple forms. I also make sugar cookies and popcorn balls, and we fill small bags for the children on Christmas Eve, enough for each child to take one home after the carol sing."

"Does Otto come?" The question fell out of his mouth before he could stop it.

Her eyes dulled. "No. I invited him a few years ago, but he's never attended. Something I said upset him, I think."

Wil had stuck his neck out a couple times in the last few hours. Once more shouldn't make any difference.

"I'd like to tell you something about my uncle."

She sank to the rocker, open faced and listening, the tray on her lap.

"Otto is my pa's older brother. When I was a sprout, his wife, Inga, made *Engelszopf* every Christmas. She gave it as gifts and brought it to family dinners and church socials until the winter she took sick and died.

"After the funeral, Otto found three braided loaves, covered and rising on the kitchen counter. He hadn't noticed them before, and by then, it was too late to bake them and give them away. They were ruined.

"He never attended another family gathering or church event. Said God had stolen Inga from him, and he'd never forgive Him for it. Not long after, he pulled up and left."

Lena had gone pale and sat staring across Wil's cot as if watching the scene unfold on the papered wall.

"Such loss," she finally whispered. "And at Christmas-time."

⁓

Lena set the tray on the kitchen table, where she returned the sugar and cream, then put Wil's dishes in the wash pan. He might sleep through to supper, the way he looked. He must have traipsed all over town this morning.

A loud *chock* sounded behind the house.

She stiffened. Again, the sharp ring of steel splitting wood.

Through the kitchen curtains she saw Tay raise the ax with a two-handed swing and bring it down on the upright end of a pine log. *Snap!*

The wood box by the stove was almost empty, something he usually didn't let happen. He'd been preoccupied lately. Or vexed. Whatever it was seemed to power his efforts, and his hair bounced into his face with every blow of the ax.

Was he worried about one of his patients? Or had he seen Otto Bergman in town this morning? He'd taken the blacksmith's rudeness more to heart than she'd expected. He needed to let it go. Besides, she didn't need him bristling on her behalf at the remarks of ill-tempered old men.

Her heart squeezed again at Wil's account. A hundred little pieces fell into place, like wood chips flying around the chopping block. But in her mind's eye, they fell into the puzzle of a gruff old smithy's life story. Of the wound he bore. Embittered and riven with resentment.

She'd had no idea the blacksmith carried painful memories of Christmas. Surely, turning his back on God had made them even harder to bear. No wonder he had rebuffed her.

Arms full, Tay headed for the house.

She opened the door and stepped aside. "Thank you. I'll be baking today, and a full wood box is exactly what I need."

"Before I go, I'll stack more on the porch so it's out of the weather and easy to reach."

"Go? Where are you going? What about dinner?"

He rubbed his shirt sleeve across his brow, perspiration shining there in spite of the cold. "I need to check on Mrs. Stanley. Her baby was a little colicky last time I was out to the house. And Joe Cooper's arm is about healed up, but I want to make sure he's well enough to return to work. He's faunching at the bit like somebody else we know."

Oh, she knew.

"While you're stacking, I'll pack sandwiches and cookies for you to take. I'd rather you returned before dark than spend daylight here eating dinner."

"Yes, ma'am." He cocked a stiff hand in salute as he left.

She followed him out. "And, Tay, don't forget to stop by Owens' Dry Goods and remind *Rebecca* and her father about the Christmas dinner."

Exasperated, he waved her off without looking back.

She went back inside, chuckling,. Rebecca Owens needed no reminder about Christmas dinner or anything that had to do with Dr. Taylor Carver, for that matter. But Dr. Carver, on the other hand, was mule stubborn and deaf as a post if he didn't know she had eyes only for him on Sunday mornings. She probably didn't hear a thing Pastor Thornton said.

As fun as it was to torment Tay about the young woman, if Lena didn't get serious about her baking and knitting, Christmas would be upon her before she knew it.

She sat down at the table and wrote out her plans for Christmas dinner.

Three turkeys or eight chickens if no one donated the birds, wild or otherwise
Ham – if the Taylors brought it
Corn bread dressing
Baked beans with side pork and molasses
Sweet potato mash with molasses
Yeast rolls and biscuits
Pumpkin and dried peach pies
Mashed potatoes, gravy
Cookies
Preserves
Fresh butter
Mulled cider
Coffee

And chairs. Every year she ran short on chairs and had to beg and borrow from the neighbors.

Without a formal table, she always set Tay's surgery table against the dining room wall with a fancy cloth where she placed all the dishes and prayed that people wouldn't figure out what held them. Maybe someday they'd have enough money for a proper dining table and matching chairs, so guests wouldn't have to prop their plates on their laps. Though no one had ever complained.

Just before dark, Tay and Winnie came up the lane, sleigh bells singing. Thanks to her food basket, he had eaten on the road, didn't want supper, and went to bed content that his patients were doing well.

Lena checked several times at the surgery door, but didn't go in. She had to trust the Lord that Wil Bergman was this side of heaven's gate, for he lay so still upon the cot, she could not see his chest rising from such a distance.

However, she'd not chance startling him—or herself—again.

Night edged closer to the house. She fed the hearth fire and banked the cook stove for morning, but sleep evaded her. Her knitting called, so she trimmed a lamp near her rocker and settled in for the evening.

The fire crackled, its woodsy warmth a companionable presence as she dug through her scrap yarn, leaving Tay's scarf for later.

Last year she'd made eight yarn dolls for little girls at the church party. This year, two new families had moved to town, their fathers taking jobs at the lumber mill. Each had one girl, but rather than miscalculate or fail to note family visiting from elsewhere over the holidays, she chose enough yarn for twelve dolls. Better to have more than she needed rather than too few. No child should be left out of the excitement of peering into a small paper bag and finding cookies, candies, and Christmas surprises—yarn dolls for the girls and wooden tops for the boys.

Pastor Thornton took great delight in hand-turning the tops during the year—a skill passed on from his craftsman father, he'd said. His wife found equal pleasure in painting them with bright designs.

The creak of a floorboard in the hallway raised her head, and her hands stilled, anticipating the next step.

He was doing it again. Trying to sneak up on her, though he didn't seem the sneaky type.

Why did he hesitate?

"Why don't you just come right in?"

Wil Bergman's head appeared at the door, sideways and disembodied. "Didn't want to intrude."

"Pfftt. Better to have no doubt you're coming than wonder who's inching up on me in the dark."

The rest of him came around the doorframe and into the room. "Good point."

"Though there really wasn't any doubt about who was doing the inching."

His boyish grin further brightened the room. How could he be both playful child and man fit to steal her breath? It was becoming nearly impossible not to give him back a smile when he offered one of his.

She set her basket aside. "Sit there by the fire, and I'll get your supper if you don't mind eating here rather than at the kitchen table."

"If you'll share the meal with me."

This time it was the grown man's earnest eyes that dove deep to a hidden room in her heart, one she'd long kept tightly locked and shuttered.

Dare she hunt for the key?

Upon her return with a tray of sandwiches, cookies, and coffee, she found a small side table centered before the fire, which burned brighter than it had when she left.

They ate in friendly silence, and when she finished, Wil moved the table aside, leaving nothing between them. His leg extended toward the fire, propped up on the hearth.

She should have been nervous in such a setting. Discomfited by the familiarity of it all, sitting by the fire as a woman would with her husband.

But she was not. It seemed the most natural thing in the world.

Tucking the makings of a certain brown scarf into the bottom of her basket, she drew out a piece of boxboard she used for making yarn dolls.

Wil nursed his coffee and watched.

Gone was her need to cover her disfigurement in his presence. It seemed to make no difference to him whether her left hand had as many fingers as her right. It certainly hadn't kept him from pressing his lips against the back of it.

The memory of that gentle kiss had power to kindle a flame within her to rival that of the hearth. And power to leave her as ashes upon the stones once he moved out.

Dousing such dreary thoughts, she looped bright red yarn several times around the short side of the card, then slipped the bundle free, tied off the ends for hands, and snipped the loops. Next, she wrapped yarn around the longer length of the board for the doll's body, attached the smaller bundle as arms, and tied it all together. Another snip or two, plus a short length of green ribbon tied in a bow, and a colorful Christmas doll was born.

"What do the boys get?" Dusky and low, Wil's voice stole across the space between them.

"Spinning tops. Made by Pastor Thornton and his wife."

He nodded appreciatively, then added a log to the fire.

The image of Wil Bergman at hearthside would stay with her until the day she died an old and lonely spinster.

Leaning back again, he finished his coffee. "What if someone was to donate peppermint sticks from the mercantile, and say, a shiny copper penny or two? How many should that person plan on?"

How did he make her smile so easily or leave her fighting the impulse so helplessly? She strove for casual detachment. "And might this person have a name?"

He slid her a sideways glance. "Maybe."

She giggled. "Well, I'm making a dozen dolls, just to be certain that every little girl gets one. I'd rather have too many than not enough."

He nodded again.

"But tell me, how does that someone intend to get to town through the snow and mud?"

"He knows a man with a buggy, though I expect he'll be walking by then."

"Mm-hm." She picked up the card and set to work again, and in no time had five more dolls in the basket, some green with red ribbon.

"They almost look like little angels."

There he went again, surprising her. From the corner of her eye she considered for the hundredth time the angular planes of his rugged face, his wide shoulders and powerful hands, so opposite from his quaint ideas of what angels looked like.

They were not chubby little cupids or impotent ornaments hung from the branches of Christmas trees.

Would he believe her? Or would he discount her story, as her parents and Tay had so many years ago?

There was only one way to find out.

Setting her scissors and yarn aside, she hunched toward the fire, elbows on her knees, eyes on the glowing warmth. Peace settled within her, and she softened her voice.

"Just before Christmas when I was four, I ran out to the pasture by myself to make angels in the snow. Tay wouldn't come with me. Said he had *real* chores to do because he wasn't a baby like me. It was a common banter between us since he was six years older."

She smiled to herself at the memory.

"And angels I made. Thousands of them, I thought. Until the clouds dropped low, and the snow fell, and I became so very, very cold."

One log gave way. Consumed with rippling orange flames, it crumbled to the stones below the andirons.

"I heard Mama's voice calling, making a song of my name like she always did—'*Lee*-na. An-ge-*lin*-a.'

"Following my snowy impressions back to where I'd started, I reached the gate, squeezed through, and continued along the fence line toward the cabin. Cold and weary, against all of Papa's warnings, I crawled beneath a bush where the snow wasn't as deep, and curled into a ball for a short nap. Just a little rest, I told myself."

Wil sat stone-like, his hands half closed on his legs, his breath held within them, it seemed.

"I don't know how long I laid there, but someone picked me up. He was strong and warm, and took long, sure steps, and wore a thick fur coat where I pressed my face against its soft wood-smoke scent.

"He took me to the cabin and laid me on Mama and Papa's bed. That's when I got my eyes open and saw him. So big it seemed he wouldn't fit in our tiny cabin, but he did. His eyes were crystal blue like the sky on a frozen day, and he leaned so far into the fire that I thought it would burn him, but it didn't. It just got bigger." She paused and drew an easy breath.

"Sir Humphrey barked outside the closed door. Mama and Papa were calling my name. Even Tay. My whole name, not just Lee, like he usually did.

"Then the stranger smiled at me and slipped out the door. I never saw him again."

A log shifted, and sparks rose in a glittering veil to be swallowed by the chimney.

She chanced a look at Wil and found him watching her. More than watching her. Leaning toward her, drinking her in with those deep dark eyes.

Believing her.

CHAPTER 10

During the next three weeks, Wil moved upstairs to the spare room at the end of the hall. So did the dog.

Doc refused to cut his cast off early, in spite of Wil threatening to do it himself. But he did agree to saw some off the top if Wil agreed to use both crutches and keep his weight off that leg.

When the land office sent notice that one of the property owners was eager to sell before the new year, he considered that clear motivation for following the doctor's orders.

The Carver house took on the perpetual aroma of baked goods, which drove Wil and his weakness for cookies and a certain baker out to the wood pile more often than not. He set up a high stump to lean against while he split kindling. And he rigged up a canvas sled for dragging logs to the porch, where he stacked them against the house close to the kitchen door.

Anything to keep busy and not go stir crazy.

Doc let him take the buggy one fine morning after Wil demonstrated a half dozen times that he could get up in the seat and down with aid of a stout stump, one leg, and *two* crutches. Amazing what a body could do when properly inspired.

Plus he had to swear on pain of banishment from the Christmas feast that he would *not* go to the livery and get on Duster.

At the mercantile he traded a half dollar for a handful of shiny pennies and a couple dozen peppermint sticks. While perusing the glass-topped counter, he came upon the very tool he needed, and told Mr. Fielding that he'd take one of those long-nosed curling iron thingamajiggers.

Fielding stared.

"They're good for more than curlin' hair, you know."

Man never batted an eye. But neither did he budge on the two-dollar price tag.

In the next case over, Wil saw a pair of fancy-handled sewing scissors. Sterling silver, Fielding said with pride. One was made like a skinny-necked stork, but Wil liked the pair with lilac blossoms around the handles.

He bought it.

After wrapping up the purchases, Fielding donated enough paper bags for the children on Christmas Eve. Said it was his usual contribution, the big-hearted guy.

Wil gave him a hard look, and the fella chipped in a small box of apples and oranges. At that, Wil smiled, tipped the edge of his new hat, and bid him a Merry Christmas.

He made his way to the livery, where he told Otto he'd be in after Christmas to help out, but he probably wouldn't be climbing up to the hay mow or shoeing horses.

He pulled a small leather pouch from his coat pocket and offered it to his uncle. "This is for Duster. And for boarding him all this time. I appreciate you buying him and taking such good care of him."

"*Nein.*" The big man shook his head, his blackened hands at his sides.

"I said I'd pay you back."

"*Ja*. But I did not say I would take it."

The crusty ol' dodger had a shell like an armadillo, only thicker, and Wil knew there was no point in arguing.

"Much obliged. But I'll help you, like I promised."

"Until you move to your new place?"

He caught the wry twist of his uncle's mouth.

"You get around."

"*Nein*. My customers talk. I know it is what you came here for, so I am happy for you." He raised one hand—end of conversation.

Wil tugged on his hat brim. It was a long shot, but this would likely be his only opportunity.

"I know how you feel about Christmas and all. But you might enjoy the Christmas Eve service, seeing what they do for the young'uns. Might be a way to honor Inga, since she was such a giving woman."

Otto's beefy hands clenched in rhythm with the muscle in his jaw, but he stood his ground and made no sign either way.

Wil gave a quick nod and walked back to check on Duster, assuring the old boy it wouldn't be long until they were out on the range together again, but a lot closer to home this time.

On his way past the anvil, he slowed. "*Frohe Weihnachten*, Otto. Merry Christmas."

When he jangled into the Carvers' lane, Doc ran out to meet him with his doctorin' satchel and said he had a baby bein' born at the next place over. The Perkins' boy had run all the way to get him.

"Sorry I took so long." Wil handed him the fruit box, then hooked his package by the string and climbed down.

"It hasn't been long since Davy left. In fact, you saved me having to harness Winnie."

He climbed up, turned the buggy, and took off at a fast clip, Winnie jinglin' up a storm.

Lena had dinner on the table, and Wil wanted to spend the rest of the day with her, but he had something he needed to do. He couldn't take dinner at the moment, but he'd be down later, if she didn't mind setting his plate in the warmer. As a peace offering he gave her the stack of paper bags.

She thanked him with her little huff and waved him off, but he caught a flash of green and the curve in her pink lips. Inspiration aplenty.

Maybe he'd been wrong earlier about bad timing. He'd managed to move upstairs in time for privacy with his project, and he'd found what he needed at the mercantile when he was buying treats for the youngsters.

Two months ago, he'd ended up along the road to town, propped against a tree when Doc Carver happened to ride by on his rounds. And the scallywags who ambushed him happened to pick his uncle's livery to sell off his good horse and saddle.

But most important of all, Doc's handsome and kind-hearted sister was not yet married.

The Good Book was right. There was a time for everything.

Like last night by the fire.

At the end of Lena's story, a quiet kind of awe had swirled around them, and his chest cinched tighter than a swelled-up bronc. The firelight danced on her cheeks and in her hair, and for just a heartbeat or two he thought she was the closest thing to a real angel that he'd ever seen.

She'd left out the hard part, but he already knew how a sawbones had come the next day and cut off a little girl's black, frostbit fingers to save her hand and arm.

Tay had told him on the buggy ride back from town, right after he'd shared how Lena, in her giving way, invited *everyone* to their annual Christmas dinner and somehow managed to feed all who showed up even if there wasn't enough food to go around.

Now, as then, Wil's hands ached to hold her, draw her close. Feel her soft yellow hair around his fingers and pour into her for all that she poured out to others.

Shaking off his longings, he unwrapped the curling iron and tucked the tiny scissors under his pillow. Then he fetched the peach-tin rings from beneath the bed and went to work. He had three chances to get it right.

⁓

Lena rolled out a mound of sugar cookie dough with more than enough force until it was pie-crust thin. She wadded it up and started over, certain that this batch would be as tough as shoe leather. But irritation had a way of affecting her baking.

It was highly inconvenient and frustrating to have Wil Bergman in the spare room at the end of the upstairs hall. That room was on the way to nowhere.

She could not simply happen by as she went to the front porch, or peek in on him after winding the dining room clock. Or pause close by while setting a pan of water at the door for the dog.

She stopped. Come to think of it, she hadn't seen that animal all day. Surely it wouldn't wander off and get caught up with a pack of coyotes. It didn't seem to be that ignorant.

Again she pounded the rolling pin against the butter-colored dough. The dog should be the least of her worries. The way Wil and Tay were going through her cookies, she'd be lucky if she had enough for the children's bags on Christmas Eve with any left over for dinner the next day. Honestly. Those men ate like mules.

Last Sunday after the service, Emma Hopkins had assured her that she'd have a plum pudding and two apple pies for Christmas dinner. Henry Finch said he had two gobblers his wife would stuff and cook.

Cecilia the dressmaker promised to drop off a new tablecloth she'd embroidered with holly, and several other people said they'd bring their usual offerings.

The event always turned into a test of faith, Lena found, trusting that people would do as they said they would. Having faith in people was much more trying than having faith in the Lord.

As the afternoon wore on, her frustration lessened, seeping away as it always did when she was busy creating in some fashion, whether cooking or knitting. The dolls were finished, as was Tay's green cap and scarf. Only Wil's gift remained, and it was nearly complete.

A creak on the stairs caught her ear. She opened the oven door and slid in a sheet of star-shaped cookies. Then wiping her hands on her apron, she listened to the approaching *thud-clomp* in the hall.

Oh, how she would miss that sound after Christmas. But she mustn't think about that now. There would be more than enough time to moon about after the holiday.

Wil clomped to his chair at the table, an odd tilt to his mouth, while she retrieved his plate from the warmer. Setting it before him, she put on the best face she could summon, trying to convince herself that she was perfectly content in her lot, and more than pleased to cook and keep house for her brother, the finest doctor Piney Hill had ever known.

Half-truths were as hard to pull off as all-out lies.

Wil sat with his hands in his lap rather than digging in to his meal.

"Coffee?" Of course he wanted coffee, but he was so quiet and still, it felt unnatural.

He nodded, a quirk teasing his lips.

She must not look at his lips.

After bringing two cups to the table, she took the chair across from him. Bold perhaps, but just as the hairs of her head were numbered, so were Wil's days in the house.

"I have something for you."

Her spoon paused above the sugar bowl. "You do?"

He reached across the table and laid that something on the cloth, his big hand hiding it.

Then he lifted his hand.

A tin figure lay before her, shaped along the lines of a gingerbread man cookie cutter. But instead of forming two legs, the bottom edge curved into one smooth line, turning up on each side toward the place where arms would be. And instead of short, narrow arms, the tin spread wing-like on each side, unfurling near the top with a round head between them.

She covered her mouth, attempting to cover a cry.

"Do you know what it is?"

Blinking futilely against tears, she nodded, afraid to speak.

His brows dipped. "Do you like it?"

Impulsively, she reached for his hand and he took hers in both of his.

"Yes. It's perfect."

Relief eased his shoulders. The muscles in his face relaxed, and his eyes warmed. "Like you."

Lena had run short on many things in her life, but never words. And now, when she needed them most, all but two had vanished.

"Thank you."

His smile said everything else.

CHAPTER 11

Christmas Eve came as quickly as Lena had feared. Her fretting had slowed it not one bit. But she was ready. And this year the children's bags held more surprises than ever before, including one sugar-sprinkled angel cookie each.

As much as she delighted in them, she also grieved. Again Christmas had become an odd mix of joy and pain, bitter and sweet, up and down. Never would she look at that tin cutter and not think of the rough cowboy whose strong, capable hands had created such a delicate prize.

The night was clear and cold, sparkling like the angel cookies as everyone filed into the church. It seemed a larger crowd than before, and they pressed into the main room, filling the pews and standing along the back wall near a stately spruce. With barely contained childish anticipation lacing the atmosphere, Pastor Thornton wisely kept his message brief, ending with mention of Lena's favorite carol.

"'Silent night, holy night,' the song writer penned. I suppose one out of two isn't bad. Unless that blessed Infant was sleeping, I doubt it was a silent night in Bethlehem's stable."

A soft chuckle of agreement rippled through the parishioners.

After a Christmas blessing, the lamps were lowered, candles lit, and the lovely strains of "Silent Night" filled the room. Several more carols followed, until at last the back pews were moved forward, making room around the festooned spruce in the corner. The lamps were turned up and women offered bowls of hot cider from tables along the wall.

Paper chains and popcorn garland decorated the tree, all the work of little hands. And two dozen paper bags skirted beneath it, awaiting distribution among those young ones.

Lena served at one table, ladling cider into cups and wishing Christmas blessings to those who stopped to warm themselves. But her focus was never far from the tall cowboy across the room who warmed her heart, visiting with the men, one a stout old smithy with blackened fingers and a shy, soft look around his eyes.

A miracle, to her way of thinking.

Had Wil changed his uncle's mind? Said something that turned the man's heart from grief to grace and brought him to the service after all those years of pain? What a gift.

As families began to leave, each child took a paper bag on their way out. Lena noticed a little yellow-haired girl standing off by herself, no siblings or parents nearby. Perhaps a visitor, too shy to crowd the tree with the others.

A woman soon appeared with an infant in her arms and ushered the girl toward the door.

Lena's heart stopped. She glanced at the tree, so gaily decorated yet missing all its paper bags. Not one was left, and the quiet little girl would leave empty-handed. How could Lena let that happen?

Frantically, she searched the room for someone she could generously rob, promising to make it up to them the next day. And then she saw him.

He stepped out from behind the men and walked calmly toward the little girl and her mother. Kneeling down before the child, he held out a paper bag. The girl beamed, as if he'd given her a gift most precious and hoped for. She thanked him and from the top of the bag plucked a soft blue yarn doll tied with a yellow ribbon.

Lena gripped the table's edge to keep from falling. Wil must have noticed, for he was suddenly behind her, bracing her with a hand on each shoulder, steadying her with his quiet strength.

"It's him," she whispered.

"Who?"

"There. With the little girl and her mother."

At that moment, the stranger straightened and faced them, his thick fur coat unfastened, a cap in his hand. Eyes the color of a blue winter sky.

He looked straight at Lena and smiled. Then he dipped his head toward Wil and walked to the door.

"Stop him." She whirled and clutched Wil's arms. "You must stop him. Please."

Wil stepped sideways, preparing to comply in spite of his first trip without crutches or cast. "Did he take something?"

Peering into Wil's worried eyes, she questioned how she could explain it to him, to *anyone* for that matter?

When next she looked, it was too late. The stranger had slipped out into the night.

Christmas Day dawned prior to sunup by a good half hour, but by the time Wil made it down to breakfast, he nearly didn't get any.

Not that he was late. It was more of a fend-for-yourself affair.

He'd helped move furniture the night before, so the kitchen table and chairs had already been commandeered elsewhere. He'd also helped drape pine-bough garlands across the mantel and over the doorways. The whole house smelled fresh as a forest after rain.

A train of young'uns showed up early with juniper boughs, their dusty-blue berries boasting alongside little gold bells tied on with red ribbon. Lena laid them down the length of Doc's table that she'd covered with a fancy cloth.

There wasn't room left for a Christmas tree, except maybe in Wil's room upstairs. But with all the rearranging, extra chairs, and greenery sprouting everywhere, it didn't much matter.

The surgery door was closed, and Doc was in the parlor busy with a feather duster and a scowl that said if Wil snitched on him, he'd break his other leg.

Didn't blame the fella, but he needed to talk to him. Now preferable to later.

Wil had assumed Doc and Lena would exchange gifts last night after the church service, but no such thing happened. Lena had been as distracted as he'd ever seen her, and Doc had kept Wil busy moving furniture.

Sensing opportunity might pass him by, he cornered Carver where he was, dusting the wood trim of a settee and a side table.

"I need to talk to you. Now, if you don't mind."

Doc paused his feathered frenzy, waiting for what he no doubt hoped was a quick comment.

Wil pulled a roll of bills from his pocket, careful not to dislodge a small paper-wrapped package. Anticipating Doc's refusal along the lines of his uncle's, Wil grabbed the man's empty hand, slapped the roll in it, and spoke before Doc knew what he held.

"I figure that's what I owe you for pasting me back together, feeding me for two months, and puttin' up with my grumbling."

"I—"

"If it's not enough, let me know. Much obliged and Merry Christmas."

"But where—"

"I may prefer whiskey to laudanum, but I'm not a drinking man, so I haven't spent much over the years. Nor do I gamble. Other than one time on a good horse that nobody else believed in, and I come out just fine on that deal.

"Paying what I owe you won't make a dent in the stake I saved for my ranch. Besides, I got a good deal with the previous owner when I showed him my coin."

Doc dropped to the settee, short on words but long on appreciation, judging by the way he worked his jaw.

Feeling like he towered over the man he was about to ask the most important question of his life, Wil took the chair on the other side of the small table and turned it to face Angelina Carver's older brother.

Lena's faith was rewarded once again. Perhaps it was the spirit of giving that overtook everyone on Christmas.

Guests were abundant, as was the food they brought, and her tables had overflowed with savory meats, sweet garnishes and preserves, and desserts of every kind imaginable. Mulled cider filled the house with a spicy aroma, layered against seasoned dressing, sugared ham, and strong coffee.

Nearly everyone from church showed up, thankfully in waves, rather than all at once, for that would have truly taken a miracle to fit them all into the house. Children found seats on the stairway and considered it a fine adventure, which left chairs for their parents and elders.

Rebecca Owens and her father brought mincemeat pies that captured Tay's attention. At least that was what he tried to make everyone think.

The single disappointment of the day was the absence of Wil's Uncle Otto. But he'd come to church the night before—a first that Lena could remember. Perhaps next year he would come for the feast.

To her great delight, everyone left happy and full, and well before dark. The perfect ending to a busy day.

Suddenly weary, not only from her labors but from weeks of anticipation, she untied her apron and draped it over a kitchen chair. Wil and Tay had returned all the furniture to its rightful places, and she had sent most of the food home with their guests, especially families with children.

As always, the aftermath left her melancholy, and she sought respite by the fire. If the men joined her, she would give them their gifts and then retire to her room.

And if she were truly fortunate, Wil would leave before she rose tomorrow morning, for she could not bear to tell him good-bye.

Pulling her shawl off the rocker, she tugged it around her shoulders, cold despite the fire's warmth. Perhaps Tay had been right, and the dark-eyed cowboy had made a difference in her. But as far as that went, she would never know for sure.

With nothing to knit, she sat idly, tipping the rocker with the toe of her shoe.

He entered without a sound.

Standing quietly apart, he watched her, not smiling but neither frowning. His pensive expression held her, commanding her attention and drawing painfully upon her emotions.

"May I join you?"

Forever. "Of course."

She indicated his usual seat. "Your chair awaits." *Across the hearth and miles from my heart.*

He pulled it closer, centered it before the fire, and turned it slightly to face her as he sat, left leg habitually extended but close enough to brush her skirt.

Her pulse leaped.

A worried line pulled between his brows, and he turned a small package over in his hands. Then he looked right at her, into her heart, and his eyes caught the fire's glow, shining as if from within.

"Before I broke my way into your Piney Hill home, my life was as dark and empty as my plundered saddlebags. But there you were, hidden inside, full of light and laughter, healing and comfort."

Without her apron, her hands fumbled to hide themselves in her skirt, but he reached for her left one and cupped it in his strong, warm grasp. It was useless to pull away.

"I love you, Lena Carver." His voice was river-deep, stunning her into disbelief as it swept her along.

"I never expected to say those words to any woman, but you changed my mind with your wit and your warmth. Your generosity and beauty."

She was not beautiful. Had never been beautiful. She began to point that out, but he continued.

"Will you marry a cowboy with a bum leg, a measly section of land, and no cattle? Yet."

He cleared his throat, then swallowed, and his thumb gently brushed the back of her hand. "Will you be my wife and help me build a life in this country, be the mistress of the Circle B Ranch and mother to our children?"

Time stopped, as did her heart and her lungs, and she silently ordered them to function as they should. Swooning upon the hearth would never do, especially if he had really said what she thought he said.

Had she heard right?

"I've spoken with your brother, and he gave his blessing, but it's yours I want. I expect you'd like some time to think over your answer. At least I hope you'll think it over and not turn me down flat."

He considered the mysterious package for a moment, then offered it to her. "This is your Christmas gift. Now might not be the right time, but I didn't see any other opportunity."

She gently pulled free of him and immediately felt the loss, the absence of his warmth and strength, his silent promise of protection.

The crude wrapping bore evidence of a man's attempt, quite unlike the wonderfully crafted cookie cutter he had made. She loosed the mercantile twine and unfolded the brown paper to reveal a delicate pair of embroidery scissors, decorated with tiny blossoms and perfect for snipping yarn.

Amazed once more by his keen perception of what was important to her, she pressed them against her heart. "Thank you."

A dog barked.

Wil stiffened and looked over his shoulder.

She rose from her chair and went to the window. Daylight was fading, but she caught a figure crossing the field in front of the cabin.

The dog barked a second time.

And she knew. "It's him."

"Who?"

She ran down the hall and out into the evening without her cloak or gloves or scarf. Across the lane and into the field, she held her skirt high and followed a silvery dog that bounded over the snow.

Stumbling, she fell to her knees, catching herself with her hands. Wil was there, and he lifted her.

"There!" She pointed to the edge of the woods.

The man stopped and turned, catching the exuberant dog's front paws against his heavy fur coat. He ruffled the dog's ears, then lifted a hand to them. In two steps, he disappeared among the trees, the dog close behind.

Wil encircled her shoulders and pulled her close against his side. "Looks like you've lost your dog."

Her dog? "I thought it was your dog."

He stared down at her.

She shuddered. "No?"

He shook his head, then scooped her up and carried her back toward the house. Halfway across the field, he stopped.

Lifting her head from his shoulder, she followed his gaze to the untrodden blanket of white near the cabin.

The image lay pristine in the snow, legs swept in arching quarter circles, arms cresting high and wide, leaving the impression of wings. Lena wriggled from Wil's arms and stood next to him, searching for a telltale sign, a footprint. Anything.

But there was nothing. Only the sparkling crystals of dry powdery snow swept into the shape of a child's imagination. She rubbed her arms, the flesh goosing up.

Again she searched the edge of the woods where the stranger and his dog had disappeared. Then she looked into the eyes of the man she loved with all her heart. The man who believed her. Who loved her in return. Who wanted her to stand beside him the rest of her life—just as she was.

And for the first time she knew that having all the fingers on her left hand could not have made life any better than this.

He pulled her to him then and gently cradled her face with his hand. How deep his dark eyes, how full of promise and hope.

"Yes," she whispered into the blue-cold. "Yes, I will marry you, Wil Bergman, love of my life." Her breath took flight and hovered between them.

Until smiling, he bent to warm her lips with his own.

~ ~ ~

Thank you for being an Inspirational Western Romance reader.

I hope you enjoyed Lena and Wil's story as much as I enjoyed discovering it.

Please encourage others to read it by leaving a brief review on your favorite book sites and social media. Just a few lines are a huge blessing to an author.

Sign up for my quarterly author update and receive a *free* book via my web site at https://www.davalynnspencer.com.

Acknowledgements

Thank you to all who aided and supported me in the telling of these stories: my early readers Jill, Amanda, Donna, Nancy, and Susan; Anke Giegandt for her help with the German language; Ann Goldman and knitting crew for their "purls of wisdom;" my editor, Christy Distler of Avodah Editorial Services, and to the Creator for His unlimited, surprise-filled, and inspiring high-country creations.

ABOUT THE AUTHOR

Bestselling author and winner of the **Will Rogers Gold Medallion** for Inspirational Western Fiction, Davalynn Spencer keeps busy #lovingthecowboy and writing heart-tugging romance with a Western flair. Learn more about her books at www.davalynnspencer.com.

CONNECT WITH DAVALYNN

Quarterly author update and free e-book:
http://eepurl.com/xa81D

Website: www.davalynnspencer.com

Facebook: www.facebook.com/AuthorDavalynnSpencer

Twitter: @davalynnspencer

Goodreads:
www.goodreads.com/author/show/5051432.Davalynn_Spe
ncer

Pinterest: https://pinterest.com/davalynnspencer/boards/

Amazon Author page:
www.amazon.com/author/davalynnspencer

~ May all that you read be uplifting. ~